Soft White Underbelly

a novella...no, a collection of short stories...
no, a novella *and* a collection of short stories

by
Ray Holland

Cover and illustrations by Laura Dittmeier

Soft White Underbelly
© Copyright 2010 by Ray Holland

ISBN-10: 0982857306
ISBN-13: 978-0-982-85730-4

Published by Great Big Dog
P.O. Box 161272
Louisville, KY 40256
www.greatbigdog.com

Some of the stories in this book have been previously published:

- "Throwing a Bloody Pig Heart Against the Wall of Oblivion" might have appeared in a 1989 issue of *Var Tufa* under the title "Throwing Play-Doh Against the Wall of Oblivion." *Might* have? Yes. It was accepted, but I'm not sure what eventually happened. That's how it goes sometimes.
- "Amelia's Invisible Show" and "Who Let Him in Here?" appeared in the Spring 1990 and Summer 1990 issues, respectively, of *Wax and Lead*.
- "Soft White Underbelly" appeared in the August 1990 issue of *Eotu*.
- "An Invitation to Everything" and "Lazy Sunday" appeared in the Fall 1990 and Spring 1991 issues, respectively, of *The Emerald City Review*.

The author has lovingly rewritten each of these stories for inclusion here—some with only minor changes, others with major upheaval—so as to create a higher degree of continuity through the book and enhance the illusion that it's a sort-of semi-novella.

Table of Contents

Solitaire America, Part 1

The sun got stuck on its way down a couple hours ago, about ten degrees above the horizon. It'll start again soon; they surely have repair crews working on the mechanism, and it'll be their number-one priority. In the meantime, I'm taking full advantage of the extra daylight. I'm sitting on my front porch with the current issue of *Modern Amnesia* in one hand and a cold can of Volstead's Quasi-Heavy Ale (seasoned with plywood ash) in the other. The clouds are playing duck, duck, goose, and the squawks of the pterodactyls that nest in the alley are particularly soothing today.

It's nice. It's relaxing. It's a little slice of heaven on earth...

Someone shakes me, and I awake with a gasp, dropping both the magazine and the ale.

"Oh, I'm sorry, sir," the intruder says. "I didn't realize you were asleep."

How could he not realize? I was probably snoring. "What do you want?" I grumble. I've seen this guy around the neighborhood, but I don't know his name.

He holds a clipboard up. "I have a petition I'd like you to sign."

"For what?"

"For a better America."

This raises all sorts of questions. Well, just one, really. "What's involved in a better America?" I ask.

"Uh, you know," he says, chuckling nervously. "Solving all our problems."

"All of them? That sounds rather ambitious."

"All of them."

"Crime?"

"A thing of the past."

"Unemployment?"

"A job for every person, and a person for every job."

Sounds good. "And what about those awkward moments when some stranger comes walking up to you and says hello, and you say hello to be polite, and then you realize he was really talking to someone behind you? No more of those?"

"I hope not," he says. "I hate when that happens. But I can't make any promises. I think there will probably be limits on how far this can go."

His honesty sells me. And even with limits, I like the idea. "Let me have that petition."

He hands it over, along with a pen. I start to sign but then hesitate. The thought strikes me that maybe I don't want my name associated with this. If it backfires—if there's an investigation—I could turn up in any number of databases as some sort of subversive. Who needs that? I scrawl *Les*

Izmore on the first empty line, just below *Rosie Cheeks*, and hand the petition back to the guy. I hope he doesn't notice that my mailbox has the name **THOR** painted on it.

"Thank you, Mr. Izmore," the guy says.

"What's your name?" I ask.

"I'm Stanley Dirndl," he says, offering his hand.

I give him a weak, unenthusiastic handshake. "Can I ask what inspired you to do this?"

He smiles. "May I sit down?"

Oh, geez. I shouldn't have asked. I expected a twenty-five-words-or-less answer, and now it looks as if he wants to tell me a freakin' story. I don't want this guy hanging out here. It's not that I don't like him. It's just that he smells funny. He smells like...butter. Not that it's unpleasant, but it's sure as hell unnatural. It's distracting. Besides, I can't doze if he's blabbing away in my ear with a bunch of stuff I probably don't care about. "Sure," I say. I'm too polite for my own good.

He moves the other chair around and sits next to me. "I used to work down at The Old Minton Schoolyards, testing popcorn." The mention of popcorn, along with the smell of butter, gives me a craving.

"Sweet gig," I say. The Old Minton Schoolyards is a surprisingly nice facility. The New Minton Schoolyards is worse than useless. The contractors used the cheapest materials they could find, cut corners at every turn, and painted the entire place a sort of dirty-looking shade of yellow. Even the windows. Yuck. Old Minton, on the other hand, was designed by the world-famous architect Hostram Butts and built using the most sophisticated reflexive foam technology. And best of all, it exudes the mild fragrance of bubblegum. It's a joy just to drive by the place.

"Yeah. So anyway, you remember a couple years ago, when that electromagnetic storm hit, and all the colors on the planet turned to transparent orange and pink for about four months?"

"Sure. Who doesn't remember that?"

"Well, people less than a couple years old, I guess," Dirndl says. "But here's the thing: Most people don't realize this, but it had a devastating effect on the popcorn industry."

I never thought about it before, but the implications are clear. "I can see how that would happen," I say.

"It was worse than you probably imagine."

"I imagine it to be pretty bad."

"But it was worse than that."

"Wow."

"Yeah," Dirndl says. "But I bounced back. I got a job with Smerblington Industries."

"The mechanical shoelace company?"

"Oh, yes. But that was just at the point when people were starting to realize they could use plain ol' string as shoelaces. It's easier, more efficient, more reliable, and more fashionable. And at only two-thirds the cost of mechanical."

"Once again, you were out of a job."

"Right. Not only did my employer go out of business, but I lost my house, my wife left me, and the bank came and took most of my personal possessions just to be mean."

"I've heard of that," I say. "But I've never known anyone it actually happened to."

"You do now. I'm down-and-out, my friend. I'm living in that abandoned storefront around the corner on Festerville Road, where the Used Tennis Ball Exchange used to be. I have nothing to do all day but play solitaire. I can't look for a job because I don't have clean clothes, and I have nowhere to shave."

"That's too bad."

"You got that right. And for food, I'm more-or-less living on the dirt I can scrape up off the floor."

"That doesn't sound very appetizing."

"It's not. And talk about boring. The same old thing, day after day. There are only so many ways you can prepare dirt."

I get the impression he's hinting for a dinner invitation, but I really want to go back to sleep.

"And you know what?" he says. "A few minutes ago, some kids threw a bowl of melted butter on me."

"Is that right?"

"Yeah. I don't know why. But I know that in a better America, none of this would ever have happened."

"Never," I say.

"In a better America, all of us would have high-paying, fun, secure jobs. We would have important, interesting jobs."

"Heavy on the fun."

"We would all live in nice houses and eat good food and have wonderful, exquisitely sexy spouses."

"It sounds too good to be true," I say.

"You might think so, but I believe it's possible. So I'm taking action."

"You have to."

"Yes. Someone has to, and I don't mind being the one." Dirndl stands up. "Well, I'd better be on my way. Thanks for your signature."

"Good luck," I tell him. "I think a better America will probably benefit all of us. The rich and the poor. The young and the old. The tall and the short. The famous and the useless. Everyone. We're all on this weird, wonderful, wacky ride together. Right?"

***

Later, I sit in my living room eating buttered popcorn and watching the news. There's a story about angry parents who want to ban Ray Holland books. Now, although I'll be the first to agree that the man is a weirdo, I have to insist that he and his books are harmless.

But who cares about him, anyway? The important thing is a better America. Yes, yes, indeed.

Soft White Underbelly, Part 1

It's the cement goose salesman at the door. Hell, I don't think I'll ever get any work done with all these interruptions. At seven this morning, a young lover rang my doorbell. He had a gun and wanted me to shoot him in the heart because his beloved had turned him down.

Ugh.

After I dealt with him, I was unable to get back to sleep. So I began fixing breakfast. The doorbell rang again, and this time it was an old woman. "I'm the rent collector," she said. "It's time to pay your rent."

"I own the house," I said.

"Oh, uh, I mean your car rent."

"I own the car. I paid nine hundred dollars cash for it three years ago."

"I'm also authorized to collect the rent on your mustache."

"I shaved it off six months ago. See?" I'd shaved it because the rent was too much.

"I...uh...I guess I must have the wrong house. Sorry."

When I got back to the kitchen, my oatmeal had boiled over. I managed to clean up the mess and eat breakfast with no further interruptions. But then, in the shower, I heard the doorbell ring incessantly for about five minutes. I didn't rush to get it because there was little chance of its being important. As soon as I stepped out, the ringing stopped.

Okay, so now I had an opportunity to get back to work on my novel—an awesome epic of awesome epicness, to be sure, and I was in the middle of making notes for the middle chapters. It was a delicate procedure, to be sure, weaving all the various themes and subplots together into a rich tapestry of literary edification.

I sat down at the computer and then realized that since my fingers hunt-and-peck at about three words per minute and my brain, at that moment, was thinking at about two hundred and thirty words per minute, I was going to lose a whole lot of words—possibly some important ones—if I tried to type it. I picked up my mp3 player, which also records sound, to dictate the notes.

I hit the button, and blah, blah, blah. I was just up to the part where Gustav wakes up with a hangover in the bed of a pickup truck somewhere on a dirt road in Tennessee, alone, with no pants and no idea how he got there, and no hint of whose truck it was, when the commander of the Swedish army called to invite me to a party. I declined. I already had an appointment to get my teeth widened that day.

Now, two minutes later, the doorbell rings, and I'm face-to-face with a guy who's waving a brochure-looking thing in my face.

"Hello," the guy says. "Would you like to order some cement geese?" He opens the brochure—actually a thin catalog—and sticks it under my nose.

"Our basic package," he continues, "contains an entire family. Father, mother, boy, girl, and baby. They come with parasols and a picnic table, and you can order them in your choice of costumes." He points to pictures of suburban lawns with cement goose families seated at picnic tables. The geese are in period costumes. Colonial, Western, Fifties. I've never seen a goose with pompadour-styled hair before, but it looks surprisingly natural.

I look up to see a car, a late-model, forest-green Universal Motors Ferret LSD four-door coupe—a fine piece of automotive work, to be sure—stopping at the curb across the street. A guy in a black suit is driving. He glances at us, seemingly with no interest. He picks up a magazine from the passenger seat and begins reading. His lips move slightly.

"For an additional charge," the salesman is saying, "you can custom order your own scenes. Your neighbor around the corner ordered a scene with Neil Armstrong as a goose taking the first step on the moon."

"Cool," I say. "One small step for a goose."

He turns more pages. I look at pictures of cement geese playing volleyball on a lawn, of cement geese shooting a movie on a lawn, of cement geese having an orgy on a secluded lawn.

"How many do you want to order?" he asks.

"How much are they?"

"The basic package is three hundred and sixty dollars, plus tax. If you want a custom scene, we have to get back to you with a quote. We could let you know something within a couple days."

"How long does it take for delivery? That is, for one of your standard scenes?"

"Uh…eight to ten weeks." It's almost a question.

"You don't sound too sure of yourself."

"Well, no, it's just that…uh…"

"Is something wrong?"

"NO! I mean, uh…" His eyes flick around rather violently. I picture a five-year-old boy controlling them with a video game joystick, his three-year-old sister sitting next to him watching, the two of them laughing uproariously.

"This is a scam, isn't it?" I ask.

Finally, he dares a quick glance at me and then looks down. "Well, sir, yes. It is. As a matter of fact, even the cement geese in the pictures never existed. They were just Photoshopped in."

"Someone did a good job."

"Yeah. We find that most people like the pictures so much, they go ahead and order anyway."

I look at the catalog. The pictures are indeed attractive. I consider asking for a custom package with cavemen (cavegeese?), but I can't justify paying extra on a special order for a product I'm never going to get. "Write me up for a basic package, with the colonial costumes. I really like that Ben

Franklin goose."

"Actually, I think that's Thomas Paine."

"He's Ben Franklin to *me*, dammit."

"Yes, sir. Now that I look at it more closely, I can see what you mean." He has to say that. I haven't paid him yet.

I get my checkbook and write a check for three hundred and sixty dollars.

"Thank you, sir," the cement goose salesman says. "Thank you very much." He turns to leave. The guy in the black suit looks at us again. I pretend not to notice.

I close the door and peep out through a slit in the curtain. The man is lighting a cigarette. He takes a deep drag and blows smoke out slowly. For the first time, I notice his windows are up.

Well, all right. I pick up the mp3 player and see that it's still running. That means I recorded the salesman. I'm not sure how much I dictated before he came to the door, so I'll have to go back and listen. Damned interruptions; now they're literally getting into my work. I hit stop and then the play button.

"Gustav in the pickup truck. Hung over. Doesn't know where he is or how he got there, although he's actually somewhere in Tennessee." Sounds of the doorbell, footfalls. The cement goose salesman's fraudulent pitch. Maybe I should find a way to include him in the story. Maybe Gustav finds the catalog in the truck. He approaches the nearest house, catalog in hand, closes a "sale," and accepts a check. Note to self: Figure out an acronym for a company name that spells out GUSTAV so he can cash the check. The G, of course, will be for...well, for Geese.

On the recording, the door closes. Footfalls through the room. Silence for a few seconds. The doorbell rings.

That didn't happen.

"Hello, Thor," a strange voice says. "You're alone now, right?"

"Yes." It's my voice. But this didn't happen.

"All right. Sit down." More footfalls, sounds of chairs being moved. "Let's get right to it."

"All right," I say.

"You'll continue to be afraid of the economy and getting the flu," the man says. "And we want your concern over violent crime to increase. Can you do that?"

"Yes, yes, of course," I say, although I didn't really say it.

The man continues. "In a couple weeks, the president is going to announce that he's pardoning Socrates. You'll be outraged over this and circulate a petition demanding that Socrates's conviction be upheld."

"That son of a bitch," I mutter as I listen.

"That son of a bitch," I mutter on the recording.

"Shortly after the pardon, the president will announce plans for a mobile target defense system, in which all our major targets will be put on mobile platforms. Entire cities—Washington, DC, New York, Mayberry, etc., will then be able to move out of the way of incoming missiles. You'll support this wholeheartedly. You'll have to spend a lot of time arguing about the idea on Internet message boards because, obviously, we anticipate a lot of people will object to the cost."

"I can do that."

"Many people will also raise the objection that the possibility of an attack with nuclear missiles is no longer as great a threat as it once was."

"Yes, they will."

"Your answer is that *of course* it's not. But this only goes to show how important it is to remain alert. Under no circumstances can we allow ourselves to be lulled into a false sense of security."

"Certainly."

"Your major idea, when you discuss this, is that it's worth any cost that might be incurred. You'll also point out that a side benefit would be that we can keep our major population centers located in spots that currently have moderate weather at any given time, thus saving residents from high air conditioning and heating bills."

"Yes, that's a very good point. I think this idea sounds like major advancement for humanity."

"Very good."

"I would go so far as to say the government should raise taxes and hold bake sales to finance the project."

"You don't have to go quite that far."

"Oh, yeah, okay. Sure."

"Good. Any questions?"

"No."

"Okay, then. I'm going to leave now. You will

not remember this conversation or my having been here. You'll go back to what you were doing before I came to the door and will continue your activities as normal. When I come back next month, you'll immediately go into a hypnotic trance. Understand?"

"Yes."

"Very good." More footfalls, door sounds.

I've been hypnotized.

***

Industrial Waste, my roommate, comes home about an hour later. He showed up at my door one day about six months ago, saying he was supposed to meet someone. I invited him in to wait. The friend hasn't shown up yet. "Any day now," Industrial keeps saying. Yeah, whatever.

And now, he shuffles into the kitchen. He throws the refrigerator door open with a ceremonial-looking flourish and pokes his head inside. "I need beans," he says.

"I've been hypnotized," I say.

"Cool," Industrial says, popping a beer open. "Where are the beans?"

"Listen to this." I turn on the mp3 player and start the recording.

Industrial listens intently. He peels open a stick of gum, puts it in his mouth, and chomps on it a few times. Then he takes a huge swig of beer and holds it in his mouth while he chews the gum some more.

On the recording, the man is telling me about the mobile target defense system. Industrial swallows and says, "You know, that's really a very clever idea."

"So I can assume you're on board with it?"

"Oh, yes, absolutely."

Now the man is giving me the instructions to go into a hypnotic trance the next time I see him. Industrial nods knowingly, as if he's done such a thing himself many times.

The recording ends. "What do you think?"

Industrial swallows his gum. "I think something funny's going on here." His tone of voice imparts great significance to what he's saying.

"And?"

"And? What do you mean, and? Do you think I know something about it? Are you accusing me of something here?"

"No, no, not at all."

"Really? No?"

"Really. No."

"All right, then. Just so I know where I stand."

"Any other thoughts besides something funny going on? Because I had that much figured out on my own."

"You shouldn't need me to tell you this, but I think you have to do something about it."

"Like what?"

"You're going to make me explain everything, aren't you?"

"What are you talking about? There's nothing to explain. Not yet."

"He's coming back in a month. That's plenty of time to...*prepare*."

Ahhh, yes. It is, isn't it?

"Now, for the last time," Industrial is saying, "do we have any damn beans around here?"

***

They sit in a semicircle on my living room floor—Industrial Waste, Collier Figg, Chickenfeet, and a large, stuffed panda. For lack of a better word, I call them my friends.

"I don't think that comma after 'large' is necessary," Collier says.

The large, stuffed panda glares at him with the Hatred of the Ages. "I like it," he says with a coldness that almost makes me understand the nature of infinity. "Don't you even *think* about taking my comma away."

"I'll take it if I want to," Collier mumbles, but it's just for show, just because he has to say something defiant.

Off to one side, the ad man works on switching out some of the advertisements posted on my walls. He takes down an ad for Internet-enabled dog leashes and pulls an ad for soul splints out of his satchel. I'm not concerned that he could overhear our meeting. All the ad men are thoroughly trained to ignore whatever's going on at the houses they visit. Strictly business, they are. Get the new ads up and move on to the next house. We could be planning to, like, overthrow the government of the whole world or something, and the ad man would just keep his eyes straight ahead and hear nothing.

"You're probably wondering why I called you here—"

"What did you say?" Collier Figg asks. "I wasn't paying attention."

"I need some help," I say. "Listen to this." I hold the mp3 player up, as if offering a good view of a product on a television commercial, and punch the play button.

We listen. This must be the hundredth time I've heard it, but it always sounds fresh to me. The large, stuffed, panda, on the other hand, snores softly. I step over and give him a gentle kick in the ribs. He wakes with a start and lets out a loud snort. Chickenfeet giggles.

The recording reaches the end, and I glance around the semicircle to make sure everyone's paying attention. "I want to be ready when this guy comes back," I say. "As my colleague Industrial Waste so adequately pointed out, I have a month to...*prepare*."

Collier Figg is outraged. "I say we kill him!"

"No, no. We need to find out what he's up to. Why is he doing this?"

"Right," Collier Figg says. "First, we find out why he's doing this, and *then* we kill him!"

The large, stuffed panda jumps up, spilling his tea on the soul splint ad, which is sitting on the floor leaning against the wall. "Kill him!" he shouts.

I glance uncertainly at the ad man. If he thinks

the spill was deliberate, we could all be in for a heavy fine for obstructing his work. The ad man sighs and pulls another copy of the ad out of his satchel. I kind of get the impression he doesn't care about his job. I don't know why, though. I would kill to get a great gig like his.

"What I need to do is figure out how not to go into the trance as soon as I see him," I say.

"I can hypnotize you and override his posthypnotic suggestion," Industrial says.

"You can hypnotize people?" Collier Figg asks.

"Sure," Industrial says, a casual tone in his voice, as if he were telling us something no more significant than what he had for breakfast this morning.

"Bullshit," Collier says. "You can't hypnotize anyone."

"What makes you think I don't have you hypnotized right at this very moment?"

Collier gasps. The large, stuffed panda giggles. Industrial sits back, smirking.

Amelia's Invisible Show

Waterhead's getting married tomorrow, and I'm the best man. It's an honor to be asked, and performing the duties is an art. I'm determined to bring it off with style, with flair, with panache, with élan. I'm determined to go to ridiculous excesses.

To that end, I've gotten enough beer to float an aircraft carrier, two dozen dancing girls, a stack of pornographic DVDs as high as...well, as high as something tall, a five-piece rock group called the Exploding Sperm Whales, a roulette table, a couple dozen spider plants, a jackhammer, a shrink-wrap machine, a case of Play-Doh, and four Slinkys. I wanted to get a bag of ice, but I couldn't locate one on such short notice. This best man thing came up just last night.

I was in line at the Grand Wazoo Food Mart, getting a package of four-hundred-year-old parchment so I could begin the next chapter of my novel—and a grand epic it will be, too—and the guy in front of me turned around. "I'm getting married the day after tomorrow. Do you want to be my best man?"

"It would be an honor," I said, bowing.

He said, "My name's Waterhead."

I said, "Pleased to meet you. My name's Thor."

***

They're in there now, bachelor partying. Waterhead brought all his friends—Podge, Amelia Earhart, and the Spanish Inquisition. My friends are here, too—Collier Figg, Chickenfeet, Charles Fort, a large, stuffed panda and, of course, Industrial Waste. Amelia agreed to jump out of the cake. It's not that big a deal, though. Her body's in another dimension, so we can't see her.

But that's yet to come, anyway. Since we have two groups of people who don't know each other, I decided to start off the party with some male-bonding-type-stuff. The first thing we did was go out in the backyard and have fistfights. The Spanish Inquisition beat the shit out of Charles Fort (they had him outnumbered), Collier Figg threw Podge over the fence, Chickenfeet nearly smothered Industrial Waste by rubbing his face in the mud, and Waterhead and the panda fought to a bloody draw. It was most likely all Waterhead's blood, though; I'm doubtful that the large, stuffed panda has any of his own.

Next, we went inside and watched a football game—oh, yeah, another of the extravagances I went to was hiring the 1966 Green Bay Packers and the 1972 Miami Dolphins to play and arranging network coverage. I had to; this was a Wednesday night in the middle of July. So we went inside for the game and sat around watching, drinking beer, burping, and bragging about all the women we'd fucked. During commercials, we spat on the floor and pissed on the walls.

It was great.

Late in the second quarter, Collier realized we hadn't been scratching our crotches. "Hey, guys, we haven't been scratching our crotches," he said.

So we got busy. I glanced over and noticed that Chickenfeet was going at it with masochistic zeal. Soon, a dark stain began spreading on the crotch of his pants.

"Chickenfeet, you've drawn blood," I said.

The Spanish Inquisition looked over at him. "God damn it to hell," they said, stopping their scratching. "Chickenfeet, you always go too fucking far."

Chickenfeet looked down at his lap with a blank expression on his face. I hoped he wouldn't stain my sofa.

***

It's halftime now, and I hear shouting from the backyard. I go to the kitchen and look out the window; a pirate ship is anchored in the ditch behind the house. I suspect the pirates' plan was to surprise us, but they're drunk and therefore unable to keep quiet.

I try to pump a cup of beer out of the keg and

get nothing but a bit of bubbly foam. No cans are left in the refrigerator. What a pisser. We're out of beer, and it's only halftime. Not only that, but we just may be in for a strenuous fight with drunken pirates.

I call Industrial and Collier into the kitchen. "Guys, we're out of beer, and pirates are about to attack us. Any suggestions?"

"We need to get more beer," Collier says.

I give him a credit card. "Make it quick."

"How much should I spend?"

"It doesn't matter. I'm over the limit anyway."

Collier regards the card for a moment, grins, and sneaks out the window.

I peek around the doorway to see how the party is going. They have one of those decibel-measuring doohickeys, and they're belching at it. Good.

The phone rings, and I pick it up. "This is Death," a swanky-looking dude dressed in black says (never mind how I know what he looks like over the phone), "and I'm sick of this shit."

"Yeah, whatever." I slam the phone down and turn to Industrial. "Now, what about the pirates?" Through the window, I see they're on the shore of the ditch, practicing waving their swords. "They're on the shore of the ditch, practicing waving their swords," I tell him.

"What kind of resources do we have?" Industrial asks.

Hmmmm...interesting question. I run down the hallway to my bedroom and open the closet. The pirates are shouting things like, "Look out for us!" and "Oh, boy, are we ever fierce!"

I rummage through the clutter in the closet. It's been years since I've gone through this stuff, and I'd forgotten about most of it. There are several bags of punctuation, the biggest astrological research facility on the planet, a freeze-dried swan, a baboon appendix, a little piece of the membrane surrounding the universe (I wonder if this means there's a hole that's leaking out there)...

Nothing seems quite right to handle the pirates. I keep digging, though. A videotape of Lana Turner eating breakfast (I put that aside; we'll want to look at it later—if we survive), a pond, a small piece of dirty fur, the sound of one hand clapping—hmmm ...no, can't use it—geez, I've got to find something soon. My reputation as a best man depends on turning back those pirates.

Farther down, a huge bouquet of dead flowers. Where did *that* come from?

"Oh, I put them there," Industrial says.

I had not asked aloud, but I let it pass. "Why?"

"It's kind of embarrassing."

"You might as well tell me. You know I can make up something that'll be a whole lot more embarrassing than the real story."

"Oh, yeah. Right." He drew himself up and cleared his throat, preparing to orate. "Well, you know that woman who drives by the house every morning at nine o'clock?"

"Yeah, sure." I don't, but then again, I don't really care.

"I fell in love with her."

"That's wonderful, Industrial!" I grab his hand and begin shaking it. It comes off. "I thought you got that fixed."

He looks at the stump. "I thought I did, too. It first came off Tuesday, the day after I had that dipseydoodlectomy. I called the doctor, and he told me it hadn't really come off. He said that sometimes people think their body parts fall off after a dipseydoodlectomy, but what really happens is that the part turns invisible. He said nobody's hand has ever fallen off after a dipseydoodlectomy."

"How does he know?"

"I guess because he's never heard of it."

I look at his hand in mine. "It's undeniably come off," I say.

"It did Tuesday, too."

"What did you do then?"

"I went to his office and showed him it really happened. He fixed it."

"I guess you'll have to do it again," I say.

"Yeah." He looks at me, apparently finished with the subject. I wait for him to go back to telling me about this woman he's in love with.

"Can I have my hand back?" he finally says.

I tuck it into his jacket pocket. "So what about this woman?"

"I saw her drive by the house every morning for several weeks, and eventually I fell in love with her. So I decided to get her some flowers.

"I went to the florist and told them to make me up something special. I wanted the most beautiful floral creation ever conceived. The guy went into the back room and came out a couple minutes later with this big, huge, arrangement. All kinds of flowers and colors and whatnot.

"Thor, it was the most beautiful thing I'd ever seen. I wept when I saw it. It was the embodiment of love itself. It was so wonderful I couldn't look at it for more than a few seconds or it would take my breath away. Do you know what it's like to have your breath taken away by something beautiful?"

"No, I don't think I do."

"It's scary. You can't breathe."

Someone taps on the window. One of the pirates is out there, trying to get our attention. I step over to the window and raise it a crack.

"We're going to attack in just a few minutes, as soon as we get warmed up," the pirate says.

"All right," I tell him. "No hurry."

He gives me a thumbs-up and runs back to his buddies. I turn back to Industrial. "So you got these incredibly beautiful flowers."

"Yeah. The next morning, I was going to sit out in the front yard with them and wait for this woman. When I saw her approaching, I was going to run out to the roadside and wave her down and profess my undying love and give her the flowers."

"Good plan," I say. Yeah, good plan if he wanted to creep her out in epic fashion. I don't say that part, though. I don't want to provoke what would surely be a time-consuming argument. Under different circumstances it would be fun, but this isn't a good time for it.

"But I became afraid," Industrial said. "The gods would surely be jealous of such beauty. If they saw the flowers, they would crush them immediately. Or worse, strike me dead. Or worse than that, strike the woman dead."

"What gods?"

"Well...you know. The gods."

"No, I don't know."

He begins looking a little uneasy. "The gods who...well, who do things."

"Oh, I see." I don't, but why pursue it?

Industrial goes on. "What could I do? I had to hide them. The flowers, that is. I looked around the house for a place to put them, and I finally found your closet. I thought it would be easy to hide something away in all that clutter. And so it was.

"The next morning came, and I was ready to go out front with the flowers. I was going to wait until one minute to nine because I didn't want those flowers exposed to the jealous eyes of the gods any longer than necessary. I stood there at the closet door, one hand on the knob and the other hand up in front of my face so I could see my watch.

"Then, at one till, it occurred to me: What if she was late? What if she was staying home that day for some reason? That would be disastrous. What could I do? Taking those flowers out of the closet for somebody who might not show up would be exposing them to danger unnecessarily.

"I thought about that for a minute. Then I glanced out the window just in time to see her drive by."

I hear tapping on the window again. It's the same pirate. "It's almost time for that attack," he says.

"We're scared," I tell him.

"Just wanted to make sure you hadn't forgotten."

"So it would have been all right to take the flowers out, after all," I say to Industrial.

"Well, maybe. But who knows what could have happened just going out the door? I couldn't take the risk. Those flowers had to stay in the closet."

The pirate window-taps again. "You're really scared?"

"Paralyzed with fear."

"Jeepers! This is better than I expected." He scampers back to the crowd. "Hey, guys, guess what!"

"Anyway," Industrial says, "that's how they got there."

I nod. "Industrial, I'm touched. You've opened up a side of yourself to me that I've never seen before. To think there's such sensitivity under that macho veneer."

He blushes. "I've even written a couple of poems. Do you want to hear them?"

"Let's not get carried away. I'm sure they're beautiful, but really, I'd rather stick a Bowie knife up my nose than listen to any poems, written by anyone, for any reason. Besides, we have to do something about the pirates." I turn back to the closet. Okay, let's see...a self-portrait of the

Cheshire Cat, a rubber band...

Yes! A rubber band! Those guys outside are true-blue, eighteenth-century European pirates, the "aaargh-ye-matey" kind of parrot-on-the-shoulder, eyepatch-wearing, stereotypical picture that comes to mind when someone says "pirates." They lived before rubber bands were invented. They won't understand the technology. It'll scare the behoopsis out of 'em!

I stand up. Industrial, trying to avoid my bumping into him, steps back and slips on the gallon of marbles that cascades onto the floor when the jar on my dresser spontaneously bursts. I jump over the whole mess and make my way outside.

The pirates see me and stop practicing their sword-waving. I strike a dramatic pose, fit the rubber band over an outstretched finger, and pull back. "All right," I say, trying to keep my voice from wavering, "I have a rubber band, and I'll use it. Now get back on your ship and go away."

Their mouths fall open. They look around at one another in confusion.

I aim at the closest pirate and shoot. The rubber band hits him in the arm; he clutches his wound and falls. I quickly step forward and grab my weapon before the others can react.

They watch me carefully. The stricken pirate is writhing in agony. I reload. "See what it can do?" I say.

Slowly, reluctantly, they make their retreat. Two of them help the injured pirate, keeping a wary eye on me as they go back toward the ship.

"You haven't heard the last of this," the captain threatens.

"Yeah," I say. "Big talk from a sissy who's running away."

The captain scowls and shakes his fist at me. Then he turns his attention to his friend. "Are you okay?" he asks anxiously.

I go back into the house. Industrial is hanging up the phone in the kitchen. "I called the doctor," he says.

"What did he say?"

"Nobody's hand has ever fallen off after a dipseydoodlectomy."

"But he's already seen it happen."

"Yeah. I pointed that out."

"And?"

"And he said he had been an incredibly nice guy for not charging me for the office visit when I went back to get it fixed."

Through the window, I see the pirates weighing anchor.

Charles Fort staggers into the room, drunk. My oven turns into a mound of chicken fat shaped like a gas pump.

"Can you drive me to the hospital?" Industrial asks.

Fort flops into a chair. "Screw you. I wouldn't drive you to the hospital if both my legs were cut off." Well, he's drunk.

"Sure," I tell Industrial. "I think Collier can keep the gang from destroying the house. Let's go."

Industrial hesitates. "It can wait till morning,"

he says. "No sense in missing a good party."

I pat him on the fanny in the spirit of macho camaraderie, and we walk into the living room. The Spanish Inquisition has set up a huge artificial cake on a table in the middle of the floor. We're just in time for Amelia's invisible show.

In the corner, Collier now has an almost-ceiling-high stack of six-packs in front of him. Although he's never been married, he's giving Waterhead a lecture on the virtues of golf clubs. "They'll give you an excuse to get out of the house at least one day a week," he says. "You don't really have to play."

***

The party continues through the night and into the wee hours of the morning with no further incident.

***

I'm awakened by a gentle tapping on my shoulder. I sit up and bump my head; somehow I had crashed out under the kitchen table.

"Thor, I overslept," Waterhead says. "The wedding was supposed to be four hours ago."

I scramble out from under the table. "Oh, my god. We have to get moving!"

"Aw, forget it," he says. "At this point, I think my best chance for survival is to avoid her for the rest of my life."

"Well, in that case, grab another beer."

An Invitation to Everything

He's unaware. I could unleash this thing on him, and he'd be totally helpless. They'd find him later, sometime this afternoon or maybe tomorrow, slumped over on the ground next to his roses, probably with a surprised look on his face, eyes so wide you could look in and see his childhood...

No one would ever figure it out.

He went off on me this morning, Old Fosdick next door, raving about how I've neglected my yard. "Why don't you do something about your grass? You make the whole damn neighborhood look like shit," he shouted.

Not with you walking around in it, I thought, but held my tongue. He wouldn't hear me, and if he did...well, what was the point in fanning the flames?

"That tall grass of yours is why we have all these rats running around the neighborhood," he went on. "I killed two of 'em just last week."

I knew better than that. I park in the back, off the alley, go in and out as many as four or five times a day, and I've never seen anything but the pterodactyls that nest on the garage roofs back there—his included. And Fosdick's not going to kill a rat. For one thing, he can't see well enough to recognize one farther away than the tip of his nose. For another, how the hell would he catch one? It takes him ten minutes to walk across his yard. (Understand, please, that I'm not one to make fun of the elderly; I myself plan to outlive my usefulness by a goodly number of years. But still, facts are facts.)

So, yeah. I had no idea what he had killed, or thought he had killed, if anything. But I knew very well it wasn't rats.

"If you don't start taking care of that place," he said, "the Health Department's going to throw you in jail. You'll lose that house."

Anything from here on would have to be an anticlimax. "It's been nice talking to you," I said, "but I have to go in now and floss."

But he was right. On the one hand, the imposed uniformity was like fingernails on a chalkboard to me. On the other hand, if I was going to have grass, I should take care of it. And I had to admit, letting it go as I did looked pretty crappy.

That didn't make Fosdick any easier to live with, though. He was the one who put nails under my tires last summer when I parked in front of his house. I had to—the Hardisons, on the other side, filled up the street in front of my house parking their cars. I could never make him, Fosdick, understand that parking on the street was public, and further, that it couldn't possibly have inconvenienced him because he didn't have a car. He wouldn't listen. I ended up building a driveway in back, off the alley, just to shut him up.

He was the one who took me to small claims court two years ago for medical bills. It was my fault that poison ivy grew in the bushes between our front yards, and that he didn't see it.

He was the one who...well, never mind.

***

Inside, Industrial Waste had a scrumptious lunch of fried camel humps laid out. He wasn't eating, though. Instead, he was wrestling with a six-foot spider.

"Cut out the horseplay," I said. "You're going to knock something over."

"It's trying to kill me," he grunted.

"Oh. Well, that's different." I picked up a steak knife. No, wait; I wanted that knife. I found a fork and stabbed the spider in the back. It released its grip on Industrial and staggered around a bit. I opened the door and pushed it out. This would really get Old Fosdick going.

"How'd he get in here?" I asked.

"I opened a new box of tea bags for lunch, and there he was. He jumped out and went for my throat."

"We're going to have to start buying domestic tea. This imported stuff is so much better I don't even want to think about it, but they're too lax when they inspect it."

Industrial rubbed his head. "Tell me about it."

I glanced out the back window. The spider was making its way out the back gate, fork sticking out of its back like a small, shiny tail. "One of us is going to have to talk to the grass," I said. "It's starting to get out of hand."

"Yeah, I noticed."

"I thought maybe you could do it. You seem to have more of a rapport with vegetation than I do."

"Of course. I lived as a spider plant for several years," he says. He was in the witness protection program for a sizeable stretch of the eighties.

I put some tea water on to boil and sit down. "You'll talk to the grass, then?"

"Sure. Right after lunch."

                         ***

Later, I did some work on my novel. It's going to be a wonderful, comprehensive work, packed with insight into the human condition. It'll be interesting, entertaining, fascinating. It'll make the reader laugh, cry, tremble with rage—often all of the aforementioned within the same sentence. It'll delve into the essence of existence and fill the reader with the Hope of Better Things to Come.

And best of all, it's going to make me big piles of money.

But things went slowly. The only work I got done was the word "The," and I wasn't sure I didn't really want that sentence to start with "A." (When you're as dedicated to your craft as I am, every word is of monumental importance.) So I went for a walk.

***

Several blocks away, some people were having a yard sale. Approaching the house, I saw, in the middle of the yard among clumps of neighbors browsing tables full of merchandise, a cement moon landing module and a cement Neil Armstrong as a goose planting a cement flag on a cement moon surface. It nagged at the back of my mind that they shouldn't have this—the cement goose company was supposed to be a scam. I briefly wondered whether it was actual lawn ornamentation or merchandise, but then I decided not to care. It would be too much hassle to get all those big, heavy cement items home.

Otherwise, most of the merchandise looked to be kitchen equipment, old clothes, antique taxidermy gear, and worn-out time machine parts. I didn't care about any of that, but I stopped to look around anyway because I didn't have anything better to do.

On a card table was a copy of Stanley Dirndl's petition for a Better America. I signed it *Lancelot Booboo*. And then I saw, next to the petition, a paperback titled *An Invitation to Everything*. I picked it up and read the blurb on the back cover:

This book is a wonderful, comprehensive work, packed with insight into the human condition. It is interesting, entertaining, fascinating. It will make the reader laugh, cry, tremble with rage—often within the same sentence. It delves into the essence of existence and fills the reader with the Hope of Better Things to Come.

Rats. It had already been done. Now I would have to scrap everything and start on something completely new. What a pisser!

But wait—something was missing. The back cover didn't say a word about this book's making big piles of money for its author.

Yes, and of course, that was the most important thing my book was to do.

It was all right after all! What a relief! I put the book down, and a little boy came up to me. "Hey, mister," he said, "that's a pretty good book."

"Oh, yeah?"

"Yeah. It's a wonderful, comprehensive work, packed with insight—"

"I know, kid. I can tell just by reading the back cover. Now run along."

He scampered up to the front porch and began fiddling around with an odd-shaped black thing. The lady having the sale was sitting on the other side of the porch; she jumped up and bounded across to the boy with what looked like unbridled panic. She slapped the boy viciously. "Jason, how many times do I have to tell you?" She sounded almost hysterical.

Pouting, Jason turned and went inside. The woman stood still, watching the door for several heavy moments after he was gone.

I casually stepped up to the porch. The odd-shaped black thing, I saw, was a cello case. A hand-lettered sheet of typing paper taped to it read, "$40. **DO NOT OPEN!**"

"What's in the case?" I asked.

"I don't know," she said. "I'm just a customer."

I asked around and found the real sale lady.

"What's in the cello case?" I asked.

"You won't believe me," she said.

"Try me."

She glanced around and then whispered in my ear.

"Wow," I said. "That's worth forty bucks, easily!" And it was, if for no other reason than to make sure someone else couldn't get it. I dug into my pocket and counted my money. Twenty-nine dollars. "I don't have it," I said.

"If you're really interested, I'll take twenty. I'll take ten, or five, or fifteen cents, whatever you want to give me. I just want to get this thing out of the house. We have small children."

"Yeah, I can see where you'd want to keep this away from small children." Such a thing would be terribly disturbing to a young mind not yet fully developed. It could warp a small child's delicate psyche so badly that he or she could—gasp!—end up doing the unthinkable and becoming a career politician—or worse, if there is worse. "How did you get it?" I asked.

"We found it among my grandfather's stuff after he died," she said. "An antique dealer came to appraise some of the items. She saw the case and looked inside. She gasped and staggered back and collapsed on the floor, flopping around and foaming at the mouth. It was awful. She tried to tell us something, but it was hard to understand what she was saying because she couldn't breathe very well. After about fifteen minutes, she had recovered enough to tell us not to look. We asked her why, and she told us what was in the case. It was the very last thing she said before she stopped talking altogether. That was four months ago, and she's still in a catatonic state."

"How do you know...that what she said was in the case was...really what was there?"

"Well, I mean, think about the effect it had on her. The facts speak for themselves, don't you agree?"

Putting it that way, it seemed obvious enough. I counted out twenty dollars to her and picked up the case. "It's not as heavy as I expected," I said.

"It doesn't need to be heavy," the woman said.

***

I decided to take the bus home. There was a bus stop at the corner, so I sat down to wait. It was only a minute before one came.

Now, I did not wish to cause a big fuss, but the Rat in the Cap was driving the bus. And I knew he liked to play lots of bad pranks. Would I get on the bus with him? No, no. No, thanks. I did not trust him, not one little bit. That bus was no place for a person to sit. So I said, "Rat, you drive on, and I will stay here."

He smiled very big, with a face full of cheer, and he said, "Sir, don't you trust me? I drive very well."

But he was not to be trusted. You could easily tell. So I said, "I will not get on this bus, do you hear? I will not get on, do I make myself clear?"

The rat scowled and he frowned, and he shut the door tight. Then he drove the bus down the street out of sight.

The next bus came ten minutes later. The driver was a surly fat guy. As I stepped up to the coinbox, he stopped me. "Hey, buddy," he said, "you can't bring that on the bus. It's too big."

It took me a second to realize he meant my cello case. "If you knew what I had in this case, you wouldn't be giving me any guff."

"I'm going to give you more than guff if you don't get off this bus."

What could I do? I had what was, in essence, a weapon that could conquer the world for me. And it was useless. I couldn't bring it out for a mere smartass bus driver.

"We'll see about that," I said, stepping down to the sidewalk. Maybe I should have taken the first bus. The Rat in the Cap would have let me on. But who knows what would have happened? I was better off walking. I shook my fist at the departing bus, however, to teach the driver a lesson.

***

A couple of blocks down, two rough-looking guys jumped out from behind a bush. One of them got behind me and held my arms. The other poked a knife at my stomach.

"Give us your money," he said.

"I can't. Your friend is holding my arms."

"Friend? What friend?"

"The guy behind me."

The knife guy's face went blank. "I've never seen that guy before in my life."

"Really?"

The knife guy grinned. "No, just kidding. We're good ol' pards." He reached into my pocket with his free hand and took my wallet.

"Let's take his cello, too," the guy behind me said.

"No. It's too big. We don't want to be lugging that thing around."

I was tempted to tell them to look inside the case, but no. I couldn't do that to them. Maybe, though, if they'd *wanted* to look, I would have let them.

Just maybe, I thought, watching them round the corner.

                         ***

Another couple of blocks down, a dog jumped over a fence and charged at me. He meant business.

Without thinking, I held the cello case in front of me and opened it. The dog stopped immediately and looked at me quizzically. He whimpered and lay down on the sidewalk. A bit of drool oozed from the corner of his mouth and formed a puddle on the sidewalk.

I could see the will to live escape his body like steam rising from a cup of hot tea.

It worked! I really had a vision of the future in a cello case!

I must have stood there for a full minute, holding that case out in front of me, before I realized I had better close it before some innocent person came along and got a look.

***

And now, there's Old Fosdick, out in his backyard tending to his roses as I come up the alley. I see that Industrial has talked to the grass. It's now short and smart looking. Nice job.

"You'd best clear all that crap off of your patio," Fosdick snarls. "It's an eyesore."

Yeah, "all that crap" is nothing more than a small pile of bicycle parts. Industrial's been making a circuit of the neighborhood collecting them on trash pickup days for his project to build a heart-lung machine. It's not as bad an eyesore as that old statue with the broken-off arms that Old Fosdick has on his own patio. "Hey, Fosdick," I want to say. "I have something to show you."

Could I? Surely I could get away with it. If the police suspected me, which they probably wouldn't, how could they prove anything?

Oh, would life be so much better! It would be terribly difficult to do it, but life would be so much better!

Just open the case and hold it out in front of me. He would look. Even if he didn't want to, he would at least give it a quick glance by reflex. What could be simpler?

My finger tickles at the middle clasp. Fosdick keeps working, unaware.

How would the police find out what I had done? The hard way, if at all. And how could anyone introduce it as evidence in court? They couldn't. It was all so elegant!

But I'm not quite as angry now. I look over at the little castle the elves have built in the corner of my yard and then back at Fosdick. Perhaps it's enough just to have the power. The next time he goes off on me, I can smile to myself, knowing I could do something about it if I really wanted.

Somehow, that makes it easier.

Fosdick looks up. "You better not be going to play no electric guitar till all hours of the night."

My finger eases off the clasp. "Don't worry."

I go inside and find Industrial Waste wrestling a seven-foot beetle.

Soft White Underbelly, Part 2

Crafty me. A month later, my friends have snuck in through the back door, and they're cleverly hidden around the house so we can ambush that daggone hypnosis guy. Industrial Waste is curled up in a little ball under a kitchen chair. Chickenfeet has painted himself light brown to match the paneling and is standing flat against the wall, invisible. Collier Figg is in the fifty-ninth dimension—when he came in, he tried to make a call with his cell phone, got a wrong number, and inadvertently opened a portal that sucked him in. I only hope he can come back to our dimension when it's time to act. And the large, stuffed panda is sitting on my bed, pretending to be a large stuffed panda.

We wait. No one says anything because the hypnosis guy might have the house under surveillance with sophisticated audio equipment.

The doorbell rings. I feel the tingle of excited tension through my gut. No, wait. It's just gas.

I compose myself and answer the door. It's Charles Fort. Before either of us can say anything, several dozen large fish fall from the sky. Having a guy like Charles around is interesting, but I don't need these attention-getting phenomena going on right now. I grab his shirtsleeve and jerk him in, hoping he wasn't seen. "Come on in," I say. "You have to hide."

Without questioning why, Charles ducks behind the sofa. An instant later, he's back out. "The dog peed on the carpet back there," he says.

"There's no dog," I tell him.

"Oh." A sheepish look crosses his face.

"Go hide under my bed."

Charles nods and goes off down the hall. I hope he doesn't somehow manage to find dog pee under my bed.

A moment later, the doorbell rings again. It's the hypnosis guy. I stiffen and throw my eyes wide open.

"Are you by yourself?"

"Yes," I intone. Gee, this is fun.

He comes in. "Sit down," he says.

I step over to the sofa. "Okay, guys," I shout. "NOW!"

Everyone rushes out. Industrial, according to plan, brings in a wooden kitchen chair and shoves the guy onto it.

"Hey, what's going on?" the guy says.

As quickly as possible, I tie the guy's right ankle to a chair leg while Industrial ties his left wrist to a chair arm. Chickenfeet ties Collier Figg's arm to the floor lamp and then ties his own wrist to the guy's neck. Charles Fort, with no idea of what we're doing or why, ties my fishing rod to the coat rack by the door. The large, stuffed panda dances around, excited.

Industrial Waste steps back and examines our handiwork. "I think we did a good job," he says.

"Good job?" Collier says, irate. "I'm tied to the damn lamp. Get me loose!"

"It's part of the plan," Industrial says. "We'll untie you later."

Collier grumbles a bit and curses. "The things I do for you people," he says.

(Of course, it's not part of the plan, and there's no reason why one of us couldn't untie Collier right now except that it's fun to see him standing there helpless.)

"What next?" I ask.

"I'm ready to hypnotize him," Industrial says.

"Hypnotize me?"

I nod slowly.

"You don't want to do this," the guy sneers.

I circle around the chair slowly, relishing the situation. The guy struggles, but to no avail. My friends aren't particularly adept at tying knots, but they're incredibly gifted at getting rope all tangled up—which, for our purposes, is far better. And today, they've done a hall-of-fame job.

"Can I put him under now?" Industrial asks.

"Yeah," I say.

"You'd best untie me," the guy says.

"We'll take our chances," I say, hoping I'm sounding like a tough guy. "Industrial, hit it."

Industrial pulls some sort of small, shiny, round thing out of his pocket and holds it up proudly.

"My Super-Duper Captain Bugeyes Hypnosis Medallion," he says.

"Where'd you get it?" Chickenfeet asks.

"From a magazine ad. Cost me a buck fifty plus postage." Industrial unwinds a string from around the medallion and dangles it in front of the guy's face.

"Have you used it before?" Collier asks.

"Shut up," Industrial says. Then, to the guy, "You are getting sleepy."

"No, I'm not."

"You are getting very, very sleepy."

"I think your friend who tied himself to my neck is getting sleepy."

"No, I'm good," Chickenfeet says. "Wide awake." He whistles a happy-sounding little riff.

"Well, I'm good, too," the guy says. He tries to whistle but ends up blowing a raspberry. "Well, you get the idea," he says. "I'm not hypnotized."

I wonder if Industrial knows what he's doing, but I don't want to question him in front of the guy.

They go back and forth awhile longer, Industrial insisting the guy is getting sleepy, and the guy insisting that Industrial is screwing the whole thing up.

And then, finally, Industrial tells the guy his eyes are getting heavy, heavy, heavy, and the guy's head gradually sinks forward until his chin hits his chest.

"Now, we have to test him, to make sure he's really under," Industrial whispers.

"How do we do that?" I whisper back at him.

"We get him to do something he wouldn't normally agree to do."

"I didn't think you could make anyone do anything under hypnosis they wouldn't normally do."

"You read too many books, Thor." And then, to the guy, "Hey, man, tell us you eat worms."

"I eat worms," the guy says.

"With ice cream."

"Yes, I eat worms with ice cream."

Industrial turns to me, a triumphant look on his face. "There. See? No one would say that if they didn't have to."

"Well, then," I say, "I guess it's time to ask him some questions." I walk a slow circle around the hypnosis guy, keeping a wary eye on him.

"Ask a few test questions," Industrial says.

"Yeah, right." I stop in front of the guy and give him a careful look. I'm playing the role, and it's fun. "Okay, what's your name?"

"Full Metal Thermostat."

"I don't believe you."

"It's true."

"You're going to make this difficult, aren't you?"

"He can't lie," Industrial says. "He's under hypnosis."

I'm not really so sure about that, but this isn't the time to argue. Our plan is in motion, and we have to play it out. "Full Metal Thermostat," I say.

"That's right."

"Can I call you Full?"

"I prefer Metal, if you don't mind."

"Yeah, okay. I guess it's more...metal."

Industrial punches me in the arm. "Don't," I say. And then, to Metal, "What's your favorite color?"

"Favorite colors are for chumps."

"That doesn't answer the question."

"Ochre."

"Deep fried. Good stuff," the large, stuffed panda says.

"All right, let's get down to business," I say. "Who do you work for?"

"I don't know. I'm a mere pawn in this huge, sordid game, and I don't know very much except what I'm told to do. In fact, I'm hypnotized by my superiors. I would have to turn the tables on them, as you did to me just now, and hypnotize them, and then go on up the line, through about twenty-three levels of hierarchy, in order to get to the top and find out what's going on."

"That's a big hierarchy," Collier Figg says.

"That's what I want you to do," I say.

"Huh?"

"I want you to hypnotize the people above you. Go right on up the line as far as you can."

"You've got to be kidding."

"Why? What's the problem?"

"That's a lot of people I'll have to hypnotize. Do you know how long it'll take?"

"There's no hurry."

"Yeah, but, like, it'll get boring, and stuff."

"Pardon me if I don't sympathize."

"Aw, c'mon..."

"Listen," Collier says. "You know when you said a couple minutes ago that you eat worms? Well, we shot video of it. If you don't do as my friend says, we'll post it on the Internet. Understand?"

Metal sits there for a few moments, thinking it over. Finally, "Okay, I'll do it."

Sometimes you just have to get hardcore with people.

Ooze and Oz
an epic of war, advertising, athletic shoes,
and plumbing

Okay, so Chickenfeet's playing with the antenna, Waterhead's playing with the color balance, the Spanish Inquisition is playing with the vertical hold, Collier Figg is playing with the volume, and the large, stuffed panda is playing with a knob that doesn't do anything but looks pretty cool nonetheless.

I wish I had a beer, but I can't get up because the program's starting.

"Welcome to World Championship War. I'm your announcer, Lance Megaton, and boy, do we have some action for you today."

It's a big grudge match, with Canada, Italy, and Cambodia on one side, and Finland, Argentina, and Egypt on the other. Last week, Italy pulled a surprise attack on Argentina, Finland's best friend, because Canada had put a three-billion-dollar bounty on them. During the attack, Finland jumped in to help Argentina, and then Cambodia jumped in to help Italy. Argentina had already been pretty well wiped out, so it amounted to just Finland against Italy and Cambodia. Bad scene. So Finland and Argentina enlisted Egypt as a third partner and challenged the others to a match.

"This is gonna be good," the Spanish Inquisition says, opening a beer.

Collier Figg takes off his shoes. "I bet somebody changes sides," he says. "Probably Norway."

"I wonder about Egypt joining in like this," I say. "What do they have to gain?"

"We're gonna mash 'em into the ground," Canada is shouting. Indonesia, standing next to Canada, leans over in front of them. "That's" BLEEP "ing right! We're the biggest, baddest, meanest" BLEEP BLEEP "'ers on Earth! And anybody who doesn't think so can declare war on us and get their" BLEEP "kicked!" Italy leans in from the other side. "Anybody who" BLEEP "s with us is gonna end up smeared all over the battlefield! Miles and miles of bodies scattered on the ground! We're fierce! We're ferocious! We'll fight to the last man!"

The large, stuffed panda comes in from the bathroom. "Your toilet's stopped up," he says.

"I'll take care of it," Industrial Waste says, getting up.

"It can wait," I tell him. "Don't you want to see the match?"

"It's overflowing," the large, stuffed panda adds.

"By now, it's probably done all the damage it's going to do," I say. This isn't the kind of thing we should have to deal with now. So I choose not to.

"Commercials are on," Industrial says. "I'll go

look real quick." And he's gone. No patience, these young guys.

"Mommy," a kid says on TV, "he followed me home. Can we keep him?"

"Oh, honey," mommy says, "I don't think so. We don't know where he's been. There's no telling what kind of diseases he could have."

"WAAAAAAAAAAAAAAAAAAAAAHHH!"

Announcer's voice-over: "How many times has this happened at your house? Well, the Mountebank Corporation has the solution to those ten-year-old broken hearts. The X15 Home Electron Microscope will allow you to perform all types of scientific and medical analyses right in your own basement. No longer will you have to wonder what diseases that strange animal has. You can find out in a matter of minutes."

Mommy: "I'm sorry, dear, but he has hepatitis and encephalitis, and I think I saw a flea on his neck. He'll have to go."

Announcer: "The Mountebank X15, the official electron microscope of the National Goalball League, is now available at most local drugstores. Purchase before April twentieth and receive a coupon for a free caramel-flavored dishrag."

Industrial comes back in. "It's still overflowing," he says. "I don't know what's wrong."

"Did you do anything?"

"I took some bath towels and made a dam across the doorway."

"The water'll soak through the towels in a matter of minutes."

"I know that. I covered it with the rubber bath mat."

"Good thinking, man. Now sit down. The war's about to start."

Already, Bulgaria is pounding the stuffing out of Argentina. Switzerland, the referee, is trying to watch closely, but Nepal is distracting them, buzzing helicopters around the border.

"I wonder if Austria will use that weapon that makes people unable to understand language," Chickenfeet says.

"Oh, yeah!" Waterhead says, excited. "They've got to. It's set up perfect. The scientist in charge of inventing it defected from Argentina."

"Besides, that weapon was outlawed," Collier says. "The federation made a real big deal about declaring it illegal."

"Then we'll see it," Chickenfeet says. "No doubt about it."

Argentina is trying to get to the corner to tag Afghanistan in, but Italy has cut them off with relentless fire from a tank battalion. Ireland pulls some more air moves to distract Switzerland, enabling Canada, illegally but unnoticed, to lob in some mortar shells.

Egypt shouts at Switzerland. "Hey, pinheads! Watch Canada!"

Switzerland, angry at the insult, goes over to talk to Egypt. Meanwhile, Rwanda and Thailand both open fire with howitzers.

"Aw, man..." Industrial says, dismayed.

Lance Megaton is outraged. "I can't believe

they're getting away with that!"

Switzerland turns around and sees the manned howitzers. "We're just getting them ready for when we tag in," Canada says, all innocent.

Switzerland is clearly not convinced, but there's no rule against having guys stand by the guns. "I'm gonna be watching you," Switzerland says.

"Sure, okay," New Zealand says, full of the arrogance of "yes, we're cheating, and you can't do anything about it."

"With this lull in the action," Lance Megaton says, "we're going to break for a commercial."

The picture cuts to basketball star Ralph Dribble. "I wouldn't be caught dead in anything but Turbo MegaJumps. And when I dress for a game, I make sure I have an extra pair in my locker, so I'm covered in case of a breakdown."

A teammate enters the picture. "Ralph, I just use these old-fashioned TS-100 ElectroStreams. They're one-third the price of your shoes, and I don't have to buy batteries or worry about mechanical breakdowns. My only problem is the occasional leak."

Ralph shakes his head condescendingly. "Billy, Billy, Billy. Who's the superstar here, and who's the Average Joe who has to remind the coach what his name is when he shows up for training camp every year?"

The teammate, abashed, looks at his feet. "You're right, Ralph. My shoes are holding me back."

The Spanish Inquisition sighs. "In my day, it

was enough just to get shoes that fit properly."

Chickenfeet and Industrial snicker, but you have to cut the Spanish Inquisition some slack. They're much older than the rest of us.

"The rubber pressure hoses on those Air-Streams are notorious for coming off after a few days," Chickenfeet says.

"Epoxy, man," Collier tells him. "Glue the suckers in place."

"I tried that," Waterhead says. "They're so small, I ended up getting them all stopped up with glue."

"The Turbos are great," Waterhead says, "but you have to find a good mechanic and have them tuned up about once a month."

"Yeah, well, that's ninety bucks a month I'd rather spend on beer," Collier Figg says.

"During the commercial," Lance Megaton announces, "Brazil tagged in. They're continuing the relentless pounding of poor Canada."

The ad guy—a substitute, not the regular ad guy—lets himself in with his skeleton key and begins work. He replaces the ad for foam rubber drumsticks with an ad for a movie about an invisible guy who lives in an invisible house. If I were going to make a movie with a very low budget, I'd be inclined to do something like that.

Our attention is drawn back to the war. Panama looks very, very woozy, about to give out, but the tide can turn quickly in these wars.

The phone rings. I ignore it, gripped by the gripping drama on the screen. Argentina's desperately reaching for the corner of the battlefield, and Libya is trying to tag in.

The phone keeps ringing.

"Thor, get the damned phone before I kick your face in," the Spanish Inquisition says.

Well, that seems incentive enough. I pick up the receiver, and the caller is a swanky-looking dude dressed in black (don't ask how I know what he looks like over the phone). "This is Death," he hisses, "and I'm sick of this shit."

"Not again," I sigh, hanging up.

On television, a promo for a news show: "To-night at eleven: A local man circulates a petition for a Better America. See an exclusive interview with Stanley Dirndl—only on the Legitimate Information and Editorial Station!"

"Damned malcontent," the ad man mutters. "Fucking communist. If he came to me with that petition, I'd punch him in the motherfucking ear. Rabble-rouser."

Iraq is still trying to tag in. It's strange, though. Egypt's just kind of hanging around in the background, not appearing too terribly interested. Hmmm.

"Move. I can't see the TV," Chickenfeet says.

The ad guy turns around. "I can fine you for interfering with my work," he says. The regular ad guy is more laid back, more friendly. Substitutes are often like this, though. Stern, no sense of humor. Often, people resent having to allow advertisements in their houses, and they take it out on the ad guys. The substitutes, not knowing how a homeowner will treat them, have to make it clear at the outset that they're not going to put up with any guff. But I don't want to cause trouble. The way I see it is that if we have to allow it, we might as well make it as easy as possible for all concerned.

A trickle of water makes its way in from the hallway. "Your dam's overflowing," I tell Industrial.

The ad guy, curious, follows the trickle upstream. He comes back a minute later. "I can't replace the ads in your bathroom with that flood in there," he says. He takes a pad from his shirt pocket and begins writing. "I'm going to have to issue you a citation for obstruction of the duties of an ad guy."

"Aw, c'mon, it's not that bad," I say.

He awkwardly lifts a foot. "I have Oppenheimer Atomic Modulation Sneakers," he says, waving his rather large, bulkily shod foot around. "If these babies get the least bit wet, the onboard computer will short out, causing a low-level nuclear reaction that'll melt the neighborhood and evaporate the soul of everyone within a five-mile radius."

"I think I'd rather pay the fine," I say. I don't care if the neighborhood gets melted, but I don't want my soul evaporated. I'll need it after I die.

"Why do you wear shoes like that?" the Spanish Inquisition snarls.

"Comfort. They're the most comfortable shoes I've ever worn. It's like walking on a field of cotton candy."

Mongolia does it. Their manned howitzers open up with special shells containing the dreaded language-confusion gas. The opposite side of the battlefield is covered with a zebra-puke colored haze. The good guys—the Algerian, Turkish, and Jamaican soldiers—stagger around in utter confusion, babbling incoherently. Iceland, Belgium, and Cuba laugh and slap one another on the back. They've done it.

"It had to happen," the large, stuffed panda says.

"I can't believe you watch that trash," the ad guy says. "It's all fake. You know it's all fake."

"It's real to *me*," Waterhead says.

The ad guy hands me the citation. "You have a choice. You can mail in the fine within thirty days. If you don't, you have to appear in court on August fifteenth."

"Okay," I say. "I'm sorry about the flood."

"I know you couldn't help it, but rules are rules," he says.

Collier Figg jumps out of his chair. "Look!" he shouts, pointing at the TV.

A Mexican soldier stumbles out of the haze of the dreaded language-confusion gas and makes his way to the front. The Greeks, South Africans, and Bolivians are so giddy with victory they don't notice him. He bravely plunges into their midst.

"Look what he's wearing!" Collier shouts.

"Oh, my god!" the ad guy says.

I look; the soldier appears normal enough to me—that is, considering he's been through a war

against vicious enemies and was poisoned by a gas
that prevents him from understanding speech. In
fact, he looks considerably more normal than I
ever have after such an experience.

Everyone is rapt. I sneak a glance at the ad guy;
his mouth hangs open. The Polish soldier, clearly
at the end of his strength, makes his way, step by
torturous step, through the crowd of celebrating
victors. Beer cans fly past his head; he stumbles
over rocks. On he goes, deeper into enemy territo-
ry. Obviously, something's going to happen.

Lance Megaton is puzzled. "A single Vietnam-
ese soldier is walking through the crowd of Japa-
nese, Syrian, and Yugoslavian soldiers! What the
hell does he think he's doing? If they notice him,
they'll tear him limb from limb!"

But they don't. He looks so intent upon his mis-
sion, whatever it might be, that I have to consider
the possibility that he's preventing them from no-
ticing him be the sheer force of will power.

Finally, he stops by a pond, almost dead center
in the festive crowd of celebrating soldiers. He sits
down, opens his canteen, and scoops water into it.
Lance Megaton is silent.

The lone soldier takes a deep breath, makes the
sign of the cross, and pours water over his sneakers.

Something's Missing

Collier Figg's mother is coming to town.

You might not think Collier would be senti-
mental about his mother—or about anything, for
that matter—but yes indeed, the mere thought of
a visit from dear ol' mom brings a tear to his eye. "I
love my mother," he says. "You know, she taught
me to..." he stops, a puzzled look on his face.

"To what?"

"Well, I can't think of anything offhand, but I'm
sure she must have taught me something. I think
she might have taught me how to heat up water in
the microwave for a cup of tea."

"Well, that's something," I say.

He frowns. "No, not really. Come to think of it,
I believe my uncle Fleak taught my brother to heat
up water, and then I learned when I saw my brother do it."

"But still," I say.

"But still, my mother is my mother. And I hav-
en't seen her in sixteen years."

"Since you were twelve?" Industrial Waste
asks.

"Yeah."

"But you lived at home with your parents until you were twenty-one."

"Sure, but, I mean...well, that last nine years, we just sort of never saw each other around the house."

Industrial scowls.

"It's possible," Collier says defensively. "It's possible."

***

Mrs. Figg's plane is due at two o'clock in the afternoon. I drive Collier to the airport—he insists we arrive at noon, just to make sure, in case the flight is early, so that his mother won't have to wait. "After all, she *is* my mother," he says.

"I know." And then, to emphasize, I lie: "I would do exactly the same thing."

We walk through the concourse. Near the gate, Collier spots a diner. "Let's go there and get a cup of coffee," he says. "See, we can sit at a table and watch for the plane to arrive."

"Sounds good."

I follow Collier as he makes for the diner. "Two cups of coffee," he tells the lady at the counter. She turns and reaches for cups, and then Collier says, "No, wait. Do you have tea?"

"Sure," she says.

"Can you heat up a cup of water? Do you know how to do that, in the microwave?"

"Sure," she says. "Believe it or not, they train

us pretty well."

"Good. So, can you do that, and give me a tea-bag?"

"I don't think so," she says. "I don't think we have teabags. We just have that big machine that makes tea."

"Oh. Coffee, then."

The lady pours two cups of coffee and puts them on the counter. "That'll be three dollars," she says.

"And a bag of potato chips," Collier says.

She looks at the display thingy with bags and bags and bags of bagged snacks clipped to it. From where I stand, I can see fried hummingbird tongues, rebaked squid liver balls, dehydrated rooster combs (in regular, sour cream and onion, and jalapeno flavors), and a host of other wholesome and nutritious snacks. I don't, however, see any—

"I'm sorry, sir, but we're out of potato chips," she says.

"How can you be out of potato chips?" Collier asks.

"Our shipment didn't come this morning."

Collier gives her a suspicious look. As she steps away to wait on another customer, he leans in close to me and whispers, "I think she's holding out on us."

"Holding out? Why?"

"She's hoarding them. You know, Thor, when the final breakdown of society comes, and there's no more law and order, money will be worthless. Potato chips will be the new currency."

"Well—"

"Mark my words," he says. "It's going to happen, and it's not that far away. Either she's hoarding them herself, or the shipment didn't come because the truck was hijacked."

"Collier, I think you've finally gone off the deep end."

"Not to worry, my friend." He gives the lady—now occupied with other customers—a dirty look. "When you wake up one morning and look out your window and see rioting in the streets, call me. That is to say, call me if there's still phone service. I'll protect you."

"I will."

A teenage girl bops up to us. "Excuse me, sirs, would you like to sign a petition asking the government for a Better America?"

"Yes, certainly," Collier says. "It might just prevent the final breakdown of society from happening. Hand that petition right over." He grabs it from her and scribbles something. Then he hands it to me. "Sign this, Thor."

"Sure." I take the petition and notice that he signed *Johnny the Human Extension Cord* in very large letters over the top of three other signatures. Seeing the names *Pandora Spocks* and *Norman Sisyphus* already on the page, I opt for something less ponderous and write *Sandy Beech*. Then I hand the petition back to the girl.

"Thank you," she says.

"Think nothing of it," Collier says. "And good luck."

The girl steps over to the next table, and Collier continues. "As I was saying, I think that woman is holding out on me. But there's not going to be any way of arguing with her."

I feel a bit reassured. Maybe he won't, as I feared, cause a scene over this.

"I'm going to see what's in that vending machine," Collier says. "It's probably cheaper over there, anyway." With that, he gets up and goes off across the concourse toward a bank of a half-dozen vending machines.

I turn my attention to my placemat, which has a detailed history of the French Revolution printed on it. France, it seems, was near bankruptcy at the time, in large part due to helping the US with its own revolution. Wow. I had no clue.

Suddenly I hear banging noises. I look around to see Collier pounding on one of the vending machines with his fists—as if, like, as if he were trying to kill it or something. He pounds on it a few more times and then staggers back. About eight or ten onlookers watch, keeping their distance, apprehensive looks on their faces.

Collier stands there, wobbling from side to side, looking like that last bowling pin that may or may not fall over. Thankful that airport security hasn't shown up yet, I rush over to see what's going on.

"It took my soul," Collier says.

"What?"

"That machine. It took my soul."

I grab him by the arm and lead him away. "What on earth are you talking about?"

"I was about to put my money in, and the machine sucked my soul in through its coin slot."

"No, it didn't."

By now we're back to our table, but I'm thinking that maybe we want to get a little farther from the scene of Collier's little commotion. "Thor," he said, "stop. Face me. Look me in the eye."

I look. And sure enough, it's...spooky-empty in there. Now, Collier's never been what I would call a "deep" individual—I've found more soulful things in ashtrays—but *this* is just plain eerie.

"Nothing, right?" he asks.

"Collier, I don't know what to say."

"That's because there's nothing to say."

We walk through the concourse for a few minutes. His mother's plane isn't due for another hour and a half.

"What are you going to do about it?" I ask.

"I'm not sure what you mean."

"If that machine took your soul, don't you want it back? Shouldn't you file a complaint or something?"

"Oh, yeah. Well, maybe I should. Who would we go see about that?"

"I guess the vending machines are probably operated by an outside company. Find out who."

Collier stops suddenly. "Thor?"

"What?"

"What if other people are getting their souls stolen? Those machines are just sitting there, man. There's, like, a bunch of 'em all line up. Someone could be running a black market soul ring. This could be a matter of public safety."

"You think we should warn people? Maybe put up a sign or something?"

"Hmmm...I dunno. Maybe it's no big deal. Now that I think about it, I'm not feeling much different."

"Are you kidding?"

"What? No. I'm not feeling much different. Not really. Maybe no different at all."

"What are you saying? You don't care?"

"It's hard for me to see why I should," Collier says. "If it meant I had to eat a special diet or register at city hall or something, that would be a drag. Or, you know, if, as a result of this, I had to wear a special harness for some reason, then maybe."

"Why would you have to—"

"Well, actually, wearing a special harness might be fun. But really..." He trails off, shrugging. "What were we talking about?"

An idea occurs to me. "How do you feel about your mother coming to visit?"

"She's my mother, Thor. How do you *think* I feel?"

"I don't know. That's why I'm asking."

"Well, she's my *mother*."

"Oh, sure. That clears it up." But it doesn't escape my notice that this time, the thought of dear ol' mom coming to visit doesn't bring a tear to his eye.

***

We pick up Mrs. Figg, and she has a nice, three-day visit. Collier introduces her to our little circle of friends—Industrial Waste, Charles Fort, Chickenfeet and the large, stuffed panda. She seems quite taken with the large, stuffed panda. "He's so *cute!*" she exclaims in delight. By the second day, the thought briefly flits through my mind that the two of them might have a little something going on, all sneaky-like, but that's not really something I want to think about. I certainly don't want to mention it to anyone.

And although she seems preoccupied by the idea that maybe Collier—her son, her baby boy—is somehow feeling a bit under the weather, as far as I can tell, she never seems to notice the emptiness in him, the lack of a soul.

Nor does he tell her. I urge him to a couple times, but he doesn't see why he should. "I don't have to tell her every little thing, for Pete's sake," he says.

When it's time for her to go home, we drive her to the airport and see her off.

***

And now, on our way out of the airport, we walk past the sinister vending machine.

"There it is," I say. "Do you want to see if we can file a complaint with someone?"

"Kinda late now, isn't it?"

"I guess." If he doesn't care, I sure don't. It's not my soul, and I have no intention of going anywhere near those machines.

"I really wonder," Collier says, "just why I need a soul, anyway. What does it do for me?"

"That's a good question."

"It's a very good question." Collier leads me over to the diner where he tried to buy chips three days ago. "Cup of coffee," he says to the lady.

"Make it two," I say.

At a table, Collier warms up to the discussion. "Look, man, I've been watching television every night, just like normal. I've been going to work at the store and selling smoke rings, just like normal. I've been trying to get cozy with Trish, that fine babe in the flotsam department, although she won't have anything to do with me. Thor, do you think I smell bad?"

"I try not to smell you."

"Right, exactly. And I've been going out and buying things, buying the latest CDs and DVDs and digital cameras, and upgrading my cell phone every week, and putting gas in the car, and stuffing as much fast food I possibly can into myself, and all that good stuff. Just like normal. What more is there to life?"

"Nothing, as far as I can tell," I say.

"The soul is an encumbrance at best."

"You put up a persuasive argument."

"I'm better off without it."

"You might just be."

He leans across the table. "Listen to me, Thor."

"I'm listening."

"I think you should go over there by that

machine and let it take your soul."

It sounds dubious to me—a bit rash, maybe, and ill conceived. Just the sort of thing Collier would get enthusiastic about.

Not that I would normally be concerned for his feelings, but in this instance I see the need to be tactful. "I don't think I'm ready just yet," I say. "I might feel better about it if I were to watch you for a while and see how things go—over the long run."

Collier sits back and sips from his coffee. "Okay. I guess there's no hurry. I'll tell you, though: I wish this had happened to me years ago. I feel liberated. *Liberated*, Thor."

Lazy Sunday

Plato is livid. "There is no earthly reason to do it that way!" He's so emphatic I feel as if he's shoving the words into my face like a cream pie.

David Hume crushes his beer can against his forehead and burps. "Plato's right, man. You're not making any sense at all."

Rene Descartes throws the can of peanuts against the wall in frustration. "You people are the ones not making any sense! You're so…so *closed-minded*! You have no right to call yourselves philosophers!"

Plato pulls a switchblade out of his pocket and clicks it open. "If it hadn't been for me…"

Immanuel Kant speaks up. "Rene's right," he says. "I've always done it his way. It's more natural."

Trying to change the subject, I say, "Hey, guys. Did you know I have the same birthday as Sean Connery?"

"You know, deep down in your heart, that I'm right," Descartes says. He begins pacing. "You know that toilet paper should be put on the spindle so the end of the roll hangs down close to the wall."

"No," Hume says. "It's easier to reach if it hangs over the side away from the wall."

We're not going to finish this game. It's a shame, too, because I'm holding a commanding position: I own three of the hovercraft routes, I control five of the seven largest banks, I've conquered seventy percent of Europe and Asia, as well as fifty-five percent of Anesthesia, I've narrowed down the murder weapon to either the dingbat or the festoons, and I'm pretty sure the killer is Peppy the Simoleon Cat. Moreover, I just drew a full house, and I've racked up over seven hundred yards of total offense. At this point, the biggest threat is going to come from David Hume, who—amazingly—still has his full contingent of pawns and has managed to maneuver them into a fairly strong defensive position. Still, I'm pretty sure I can overwhelm him with superior strength. It won't be elegant, but it doesn't have to be. All I need is five, maybe ten, minutes—but I might not have that much time. The game is rapidly falling apart.

I should have known, though, that it was doomed from the start. They argued over who got to use which game token—who got to be the race car and who got to be the monkey's paw. They argued over how much of which denomination of money the players should start with. They argued over whether play should move clockwise or counterclockwise around the table and whether it we should move from east-to-west or in a sort of general up-and-down, zigzag pattern across the board. They argued over whether the game clock should be set to three or five minutes per move. They argued over how high the board should levitate above the table.

Yes, it was doomed from the start.

I quietly slip out to sit on the front porch.

Outside, things look unnatural. The elves who pull the shadows out from under objects are still on strike. I've gotten used to not having a shadow myself; what I miss is the shade from trees and buildings. I hope they resolve it soon.

A whiskey bottle smashes through the window.

"You dickless little piece of shit! I'll twist your head off and cram a fruitcake down your throat!"

"PUT THAT KNIFE DOWN!" Confused voices. Then someone—I can't tell who—shouts, "No, I didn't settle it like a philosopher. I settled it like a *man*."

Touché.

Of course, the police will come. If I stick around, they'll probably want to talk to me. That's not a situation I want to deal with, so I get up and walk toward Festerville Road, the main drag in the neighborhood. And I begin composing, in my head, my resignation letter to send the Philosopher's Union. I had joined with such high hopes of good fellowship and professional networking, but it's simply not working out at all.

At that thought, I slow down. If I take my time, everyone might be gone by the time I get back home.

A couple blocks down, I step into a liquor store

for a six-pack. It'll be nice to sit on the front porch, even with no shade, and knock back a few cold ones.

The clerk squints at me; it almost seems as if he's trying to grind his eyelids they way you might grind your teeth in your sleep. It hurts to think about it, so I don't. Outside, a siren flashes by.

The beer is hidden at the end of a long tunnel of electrified chicken wire. But I, Thor, am Master of Electrified Chicken Wire Tunnels. I have the certificate framed on my bedroom wall. What I'm not prepared for are the pythons just around the first bend.

I back out quietly. "Give me a deck of playing cards," I tell the guy behind the counter. He grins and hands me a pack. "Just add it to my bill," I say, crawling back into the tunnel.

Right before the bend, I unwrap the cards. Then I go on. There they are. "Hey, pythons," I say. "Want to learn a new card game? It's called fifty-two card pickup."

Surprised, they stare at me. Finally, one of them says, "Sure."

I flip the cards all over them. "There are fifty-two cards," I say. "Pick them up." The pythons blink blankly and then, grumbling, begin picking the cards up—no small feat for animals with no hands—but that's the idea. I crawl past them to the beer. It never ceases to amaze me how often that old, worn-out trick works.

Paying for the beer and cards, I suggest to the clerk that he put the beer where customers can get to it easily.

"It's an idea," he concedes, "but then we'd lose a lot of playing card sales."

***

A half block from home, I notice a large thing on the front porch. A large, brown thing. A large, brown, square thing.

My goodness.

It turns out to be a crate, about four and a half feet to a side. My name is written in grease pencil on the top. There's no address on it, though. I take a quick look at each side and then take the mail from the mailbox.

The mail's the usual stuff. There's a circular from a political candidate who wants to seal off City Hall and fill it with water. He doesn't explain why, but I like the idea. The less they're able to do down there, the better. I memorize his name for election day. Then there's a bill for the cement geese I ordered. I've already paid for them, so this bill will be a low priority.

I stuff the mail into my hip pocket and try to shove the box away from the door. No good. It's too heavy. The crate, that is; not the door. I eyeball the gap between the crate and the door. No, there's not enough space to squeeze through.

Well.

I take the opportunity to examine the crate more thoroughly. I look it over for about twenty minutes. Up, down, sides, top. Finally, I come to the conclusion that this odd thing is a crate. And it's a big one.

I go in the back door and bam on Industrial Waste's bedroom door. "Wake up!" I shout. "I have something I want you to see."

"I don't want to hear about it," he says.

"You don't even know what it is."

"Does it involve naked women?"

"I don't know," I answer truthfully.

"Come get me when you know for sure it does."

"What's the matter with you?"

"Wendell Putz died."

"Who's Wendell Putz?"

"He was the second guy to get killed in the American Revolution."

"Industrial, I would think you should have gotten over it by now."

"Oh, no. I'm going to mourn one day for every American who has ever died. I started yesterday with Eric Zucchini, who was the first guy to get killed in the American Revolution."

"I thought it was Crispus Attucks."

"Huh?"

"Crispus Attucks. He's generally regarded as the first person to die in the American Revolution."

"Crispus? What kind of name is Crispus? It sounds like some kind of snack food."

"Don't complain to me. I didn't name him, Industrial."

"He was the first, huh?"

"So they say."

"Well, pooh stains. I downloaded this list of

people from the Internet. I didn't think the Internet would lie to me."

"Just goes to show," I say. I think about Stanley Dirndl around the corner, and I wonder: If his petition for a Better America is approved, will it stop lies on the Internet?

"I guess Herman Schnauzer wasn't the third person?" Industrial says.

"I would have no way of knowing. What I do know is that every American who ever died is quite a few people. You might want to cut your mourning back to an hour apiece."

A silence. Finally, "Do you really think so?"

"Yeah. Better still, a minute. Or maybe even just one second. That way, you might get finished in time to do something with your life."

"I'll consider it."

Well, Industrial's going to be no help. What does he care if the front door's blocked, anyway? In the six months he's been living here, he's left the house twice—both times through the back door.

I dial Collier Figg's number. "I have something I want you to see," I tell him. "Come over here immediately."

"Does it involve naked women?"

"I don't know."

"Well, just on the off-chance, I'll be there." Ah, yes. There's the difference between Industrial Waste and Collier Figg. Collier is ready to take chances.

I go back out and sit on the crate, beer in hand, to wait. It's only a few minutes before Collier shows up in his Flintstones-style car.

"Notice anything unusual?" I ask.

"It's a large crate," he says. "And it's blocking your door." He cogitates a minute and then adds, "What do you make of it?"

"Possibly a short story," I say.

He looks the crate over, tries to move it, etc. We try to move it together. We can't. The pterodactyls that nest in the alley have come around front, and they're perched in trees, watching. One of them squawks as if offering advice, but we have no translator. "Have you tried to open it?" Collier asks me.

"No. How would I open it?"

"I don't see any way," he says. He stands there regarding the crate for a moment and then has an idea. "We'll just chop it open," he says. "I can get an ax."

"Maybe we should try something more moderate before we go destroying it," I say.

"No, we'll chop it open. It'll be fun," he says. "I know a guy who works at that hardware store a couple blocks down. He'll lend me an ax."

He leads me down the street. In the hardware store, he finds his friend and explains the situation. "Sure, you can borrow one," the friend says. "Just make sure you get it back to me before we close today."

"We will," Collier says. I can tell he has no intention of bringing it back.

Outside, Collier has a lot of fun waving the ax around and growling. "Don't do that," I say. "Police drive by here quite frequently."

"What are they going to do to a guy who's armed with an ax?"

"Shoot him, maybe. You have to consider that they're not going to think you look like the most mentally stable person they've ever seen."

"Oh," he says. "I hadn't thought of that."

***

We get back to my house. The crate is still there. I stand at the edge of the porch, not thinking anything.

Collier stands in the middle of the yard. He hefts the ax in both hands, holding it out in front of his chest. He raises it above his head. He squints at the crate. He clears his throat. He strikes a dramatic pose. "Here I go," he says. He charges forward and springs athletically off the front step, swinging the ax. The blade strikes the top of the crate with a sudden whack! and remains there, embedded an inch or so. Collier falls to the ground, screaming in pain, writhing in agony. After a moment, he recovers. "That was fun."

He gets up, works the ax out of the crate, and starts chopping in earnest. He chops and chops, making slooooowww progress. The wood is hard. Or perhaps Collier is weak. I don't know why it takes him so long, but finally he gets a board loosened. "Come on," he says. "Let's look."

I pull the loose board away, and we look inside to see a sheet of plastic. I take a pocketknife and cut through it.

"My god," he says.

"My god," I say.

It's ice cubes. We manage to get the rest of the top off, and the crate is full of the damned things. They're the goofy-looking, not-quite-square kind you get from those plastic trays.

"What am I going to do with all these ice cubes?" I ask, dazed.

We go inside, watch Lucy reruns on TV, and debate what I should do with the ice. Collier finally talks me into seeing if I can have it removed. I call several places, junk dealers and the like, but no one's interested. I finally find Weasel's Ice Company in the Yellow Pages. They agree to come out and pick up the crate for a mere thirty-five dollars.

"While we're waiting for them, we might as well make use of the ice," Collier says.

We take the beer out to the front porch and nestle it into the ice, and then we sit down next to the crate to wait for the pickup guys.

The next day, they arrive in a large flatbed truck. The driver, a slow-moving, mountainous guy, gets out and ambles up to the porch.

"You the guys with the crate?" he asks.

"Yeah, I guess so," I say.

He studies the crate the way a jeweler would study a diamond he's about to cut. "This it?" he asks.

"Yeah."

He nods and then waves his friends out of the trunk. There are two of them, skinny guys with long, tangled hair. They get a dolly off the back of the truck and roll it up. One of them, the younger looking, can barely contain his amusement.

"You'd be surprised," the big guy says. "We get these calls about once a month." Then, to his friends, "Okay, roll it over this way. Mark, wipe that grin off your face." He turns to me. "You'll have to excuse Mark," he says. "He's new, and he just had an operation. They drained about a pint of bacon grease out of his head."

"Yeah, sure," I say.

They wrestle the crate onto the dolly and roll it to the truck. "That'll be thirty-five dollars," the big guy tells me.

I count it out to him.

"Thank you, sir," he says.

Collier and I stand there and watch them get the crate positioned on the truck. "When they drive away, we're going to follow them," he whispers.

"Why?"

"I got a hunch."

With a preposterously loud and ugly-sounding grinding of gears, the truck pulls away. I make for my car.

"No," Collier says. "My car."

Well, sure. Why not?

We get in. Collier opens a panel on the dashboard and reveals an assortment of buttons labeled with notations such as "Tomato Soup," "286 Microprocessor," "Dead Cats," "Misgivings," etc.

"What's all this?"

"Weaponry." He pushes "Bleached Blonde," but

nothing happens. "Now we're invisible," he says. "We can drive right up their ass, and they'll never know."

"Invisible?" I say. "Someone could crash into us."

Collier snorts. "I bet you're a lot of fun at parties."

"You should know. You always go to the same parties."

He raises an eyebrow. "I don't pay any attention to you at parties."

The ice truck is at the corner. Collier starts his car and pulls out.

They lead us a few blocks through the neighborhood and stop by the roadside, in front of an empty lot. Collier pulls over a discreet distance away, in front of a stack of magazines.

We watch as the two helpers get out of the truck, climb onto the back, and nail a new top on the crate. Then they get back in.

"What's that all about?" I ask.

"Looks as if I'm right," Collier says.

The ice guys continue. They eventually stop in front of a shotgun house that looks freshly painted. We park a half-block away.

The big guy gets out of the truck and goes to the front door. He rings the bell, waits a moment, and then knocks. No answer. He knocks again.

"What do you suppose he's doing?" I ask.

"Just as I thought," Collier says.

The big guy signals to his friends, and they spring into action. They wheel the crate up to the house, position it against the front door, write something on top with a grease pencil, and make their getaway.

The whole operation lasted less than three minutes.

"My god," I say.

"Now," Collier says, "I'm going to do something that'll make you feel better." He eeney-mee-ney-miney-moes the buttons on his control panel, and his finger settles on "I buried Paul." From empty sky, fourteen thousand tons of shadowless flea shit falls on the truck.

"How'd you do that?"

He smiles and starts the car.

"You realize," I say, "that now there's nobody to haul the ice away from those people's porch."

Throwing a Bloody Pig Heart Against the Wall of Oblivion

First, they kept waking me with the phone. At seven, the commander of the Swedish army called to invite me to yet another party. Then, within the next ten minutes, it was Scarlett Johansson, Garrison Keillor, Miles Davis, Earl Scheib, St. Anselm, Buster the Show Dog, C. M. Balks, John Wilkes Booth, Claude Monet, Dexter Kroger, Sisyphus, Aristotle, Emmett Kelley, Matt Helm, and Elmer Fudd, all inviting me to parties. I accepted Dexter's invitation because he's an old friend and Scarlett Johansson's because...well, because she's *Scarlett freakin' Johansson.*

Finally, I took the phone off the hook. That was when they started coming to the door. The ad man came first, two hours before his usual time. He didn't change many ads, but what he did was pretty bad. In the bedroom, he took down the ad for the combination oil filter wrench-rectal thermometer (the kind with the ivory inlay) and replaced it with an ad for noise-nullifying contact lenses. The new ad's printed on some kind of shiny paper, and it's going to be reflecting the street light in my face all night.

Then, in the bathroom, he put an ad for a horse-drawn lawn trimmer on the wall above the toilet. The model in the ad is beautiful and almost naked. That's not so bad in and of itself, but the problem is that I used to know her. We went to high school together, and I asked her out one day at lunch. Now, whenever I piss, I'm going to be staring at the girl who laughed at me in front of the whole school. I'm in for a fairly large fine if I tamper with the ads, but in this case, maybe it's worth it.

After the ad man left, a guy from the Census Bureau came. "We're taking a random survey of random houses in this state," he said, not specifying which state "this state" was. "We're trying to determine which houses, and the occupants thereof, really exist, and which don't. Sir, does this house really exist?"

I immediately understood the importance of this survey. It would have a great effect on property values. "Yes," I told him. "This house exists."

"How many people did you report as residents of this house in the last census?"

"One."

He busily scribbled down the information. "How many people live here now?"

"Two. I have a roommate now."

"Who is he?"

"A guy named Industrial Waste. Actually, I'm not sure you could really consider him a roommate. He just showed up here one day. Said he was supposed to meet a friend here."

"How long has he been waiting?"

"Six months."

"What if the friend doesn't show up?"

"It's been done."

"Does he exist? Your roommate, that is?"

"No."

"Do you exist?"

"Yes."

"Thank you." He flipped the notebook shut and left.

Then the elves came out, as they do every morning. They like to climb onto my VCR and reset all the tuning knobs, shit in my computer's disk drives, spin each other around on my turntable, and do anything else they can think of. Arrogant little bastards, they are. I'm just glad they're going for the obsolete technology.

Now one is standing in the middle of my kitchen table, pants around his knees, waving his dick at me. This is too much. I pick him up and heave him against the wall. He hits with a satisfying (to me, not to him) half-splat, half-thud, kind of like the sound a bloody pig heart would make if you threw it against the wall. Not that I've ever thrown a bloody pig heart against the wall—or against anything, for that matter—but it seems fairly obvious what it would sound like. Anyway, the elf hits WHAM! and slides down the wall behind the coffee machine, leaving a sluglike trail behind him.

My buddy Collier Figg calls. "Hey, Thor," he says, before I can say hello. "I'm going to fuck

Wilma Flintstone."

"What about Fred?" I ask.

"Fred Flintstone is an idiot. He'll never know what's going on. To tell the truth, I don't think he's really Pebbles's father."

"I think she looks like him." I believe in always giving people the benefit of the doubt.

"I need your help," he says hurriedly, maybe afraid I'll hang up on him. "I want to write her a love letter."

It occurs to me that he sounds serious. "Collier, Wilma Flintstone is a cartoon character. She doesn't exist."

"I know that," he says patiently. "But I need your help. This love letter has to be just right."

My call waiting beeps. "Hold on," I say, and switch to the other line. "Hello?"

"Watch out for the dreaded mind-reading yeast!" Charles Fort shouts. He's hysterical.

"Charles, calm down." In the corner, a large, neon cobra oozes from the ceiling. He twists around, looks at me.

"Call the police!" Charles shouts.

"You know the police won't do anything," I tell him. "Just calm down, and I'll take care of it."

Adam and Eve walk into the room and look around, confused. They see the cobra. "Fuck you," Eve says.

Charles quiets down for a moment. Then he flares up again. "It's raining cow shit!"

I click back to Collier. "Come back to reality," I tell him. "You can't fuck Wilma Flintstone. For one thing, she doesn't exist, and even if she did, she's prehistoric. By now, there'd be nothing left of her but bones."

"Prehistoric," Collier says. "That's just the point. I'll sweep her off her feet with all the modern conveniences I have. Show her a car with an internal combustion engine. A microwave oven. You don't think that'll impress her? Thor, that woman's used to sleeping on a stone slab. When I show her my waterbed, that'll be *it*. She'll fuck my balls off."

"Collier, you're a sick young man."

"Are you going to come help me with this letter or not?" he says.

"You don't even have her address. How are you going to get it to her?"

"I'll just send it to Wilma Flintstone in Bedrock. How many Wilma Flintstones can there possibly be in Bedrock?"

Well, he has a point there.

No, wait—he doesn't.

Or does he?

"I'll be over later," I say.

"Thor, you're a champ."

I hang up and put my shoes on. Industrial Waste comes out of the guest bedroom and leans against the wall, munching on an apple. "Where you going?" he asks.

"Collier's house. He wants me to help him write a love letter to Wilma Flintstone."

Industrial spits a seed out. "When you get back, will you help me write one to Betty?"

"Sure." I've always thought she was the prettier of the two, anyway.

Suddenly, hundreds of elves come swarming out of the woodwork. They've never been this bad before; it's a frightening sight. They come straight for me.

I duck, cringe, try to climb the wall. But it's no use; they're all over me. They wrestle me down and tie me to a chair. A splinter sticks in my ass.

An elf dressed in fancy robes climbs onto my lap. "Thor," he squeaks pompously, "you are hereby under arrest under elf law for the murder of Wimwam."

"Wimwam?" I can't say it without laughing.

"Let the record show that the accused laughed at the charges. Listen, mister, you're in big trouble. Deep shit. You killed an elf, and now you must stand trial."

Well, I *am* at their mercy. I look around. Industrial Waste is nowhere to be seen. (And how many times have we all said that?) "What did you do to my roommate?"

"We locked him in the bathroom."

That serves to remind me I have to piss. If I cut loose with this annoying little creep standing on my lap, what would happen?

"Let the prosecution present its case," the elf says. Apparently, he's the judge.

Another elf climbs up and stands next to him. "The accused, known as Thor, was witnessed by... well, by a whole bunch of folks, throwing Wimwam against the wall with intent to kill."

The judge turns to the crowd on the floor in front of me. "Is that right?"

"Yes," they shout in unison.

The judge turns back to me. "I find you guilty," he says.

"Wait a minute!" I shout. "What kind of trial is this? Don't I get a chance to say anything? There were mitigating circumstances."

"You're being tried under elf law, buddy. When the evidence is this overwhelming, we like to save time by pronouncing sentence right after the prosecution's case. That way, we can all go home early." He looks at his watch. "A new episode of *The Adventures of Andy the Mechanical Pie Crust* starts in fifteen minutes, so we have to hurry."

"That's not fair."

The judge waves his finger at me self-righteously. "You should have thought of that before you heaved little Wimwam against the wall like a bloody pig heart."

What can I do? I was provoked, but if I'm being honest, no court would consider dick-waving sufficient provocation to kill. Well, very few.

"What sentence does the prosecution request?" the judge asks.

The prosecutor looks me up and down disdainfully. "The maximum penalty," he says.

The crowd cheers. This could be serious. No telling what kind of sadistic things elf law could prescribe for heaving little Wimwam against the wall like a bloody pig heart.

The judge takes a thick book—at least thick

by elf standards—from under his robe. He holds it
ceremoniously at arm's length and leafs through
it. Finding the proper page, he reads to himself,
trying his best to look solemn. His lips move. The
crowd is hushed. Finally, he finds the penalty.

"According to elf law," he intones, "you are
hereby sentenced to have sex with a human woman once a night, every night for the next month."

Huh?

Yeah!

The crowd cheers. The prosecutor is ecstatic,
and so am I. I don't know how they'll get her to
agree to it—after all, I'm sure most women would
take offense at the notion that fucking them would
be a punishment. Maybe they'll use the Collier
Figg method: lie to her shamelessly. Will it be
a different woman each night? In any case, I'm
ready to take my punishment and pay my debt to
elf society. I'm not one to avoid responsibility for
my actions.

"That'll teach that scum to fuck with us!" he
shouts gleefully. "Fucking a human woman. The
most degrading, vile, disgusting, horrible thing
that could possibly happen to an elf..." His face
falls as he realizes. He turns to the judge. "Wait a
minute," he says, voice shaky. "That's no punishment for him," he shouts, petulantly stomping his
little feet on my thigh. The crowd is now hushed. I
hope they don't change the sentence.

"I can't help it," the judge says. He's very apolo-
getic and obviously distressed. "Sentence has been
passed, and it must be carried out."

Yes, your honor. We mustn't make a mockery of elf law.

The elves begin booing. "My hands are tied," the judge tells them. "It's in the book."

They rush him. Elves swarm up my legs and over my lap. It tickles. The judge tries to make a break for it, but it's no use. Thousands of elves are on the floor surrounding the chair; he has no place to go. He's pushed over the edge and disappears into the angry mob.

I'm a bit fearful now. When they get finished with the judge, they'll have a score to settle with me. And I'm helplessly tied to the chair. Not only that, but it appears as though they're not going to carry out the sentence.

Suddenly, a tiny bugle calls from the other room. A large group of armed elves in uniform rush in on horses. It's the Elf National Guard!

The guardelves charge into the riot, swords flashing, guns firing. It's incredibly noisy and violent, but the guardelves are impressively well trained and efficient. In only a couple minutes, they have the situation under control. Several tiny horse-drawn paddy wagons ferry arrested elves off to wherever they lock them up.

It's fascinating, this little show going on down there in front of me. And I don't realize until they're taking the last of the prisoners away that I'm still tied up. "Hey," I say, "are you guys going to untie me?"

One of the guardelves looks back over his shoulder at me. "Oh, yeah," he says, as if it hadn't occurred to him—as if it's still not *really* occurring to him—to untie me. "We'll be right back."

***

It's been two hours, and they still haven't come back. After the noise died down, Industrial Waste banged on the bathroom door for a few minutes and then gave up. I can't figure out how they got him locked in there; the door has no lock.

The phone rings. The answering machine gets it, and I hear Collier's voice. "Hey, Thor, where are you? I need to get this letter written today. I guess you're on your way over, eh?"

The Air-Conditioned Nightmare

ishakethespidersoutofthefryingpanandploppapa
tofbutterintomeltiwalkovertotherefrigeratorand
takeoutacartonofeggshowmanydoyouwantiaskin
dustrialwasteidliketwoscrambledhesaysigetabo
wlfromthecabinetshakethespidersoutandbreakf
oureggsintoitiaddsomemilkandbeatthemwithaf
orkthedoorbellringscanyoucooktheseupwhileige
tthedoorisaysurehesaysandtakesthebowlovertot
hestoveinoticeheflicksaspideroutofthefryingpan
asileavetheroomtheguyatthedoorwearsacheaps
uitandcarriesathickbriefcasehellohesaysithinkt
hefirstthingyouneedhereissomespacesbetweeny
ourwordsbeforeyourreadersgetfedupwithtryingt
omuddlethroughthissolidblockoflettersidonthav
eanyitellhimthatswhyimherehesaysmayicomein
yesofcourseileadhimintothediningroomandhepu
tshisbriefcaseonthetableheopensthebriefcasean
dshowsmeseveralsheetsofplainwhitepaperthese
arepremiumgradespaceshetellsmefromthealexa
nderspacemillinkansascitytheynormallysellfort
hreedollarsperthousandbutthesehavebeenrepos
sessedicanletyouhavethemforhalfpricethatsagood

dealinormallybuybutlerspacesatfourdollarstheyr
enotquiteasgoodnotas   durablebuttheyreeasierto
usebecauseofthebevelededgesidlikefiftydollarsw
orthisayashehandsmethespaces and i put them in
the next thing you want is some carriage returns
he says i have some very fine franklin whittaker
hollow core carriage returns with the reinforced
right edge i have the twenty thirty and forty gauge
but some guy named maples bought all my fifty
gauge returns this morning ill have some more
within a week though thats okay i say i know maples and the stuff he writes requires the fifty gauge
but i usually get the twenty or thirty fine he says
taking a handful of tiny plastic containers out of
the briefcase theyre five dollars for each box of two
hundred i open a box and examine the carriage returns they look very good give me ten boxes i say
he counts out the other nine and i carefully put
one in place

    what else do you have i ask

    a full line of punctuation he says and of course
tabs and upper case letters

    can i see a tab

    he takes a plastic bag out of the briefcase and
hands it to me these tabs are handmade by a guy
in switzerland he puts a special pad on the bottom
so the tab doesnt slip out into the left margin he
hands me one and says put it in and jiggle it youll
find that its stays more firmly in place than any
tab youve ever used

    i take the tab place it and jiggle it

    see he says

what kind of material is that

its some kind of waste from a factory he lives close to he was walking through the alley one day and noticed it sticking out of a dumpster he thought it looked just like the stuff he needed for tabs

thats interesting i say the doorbell rings excuse me i say ill be right back

the guy at the door is short and chubby with black hair hi he says my name is willie the brain and im interested in the postal clerk job you have advertised in the paper

come on in i say i lead him into the kitchen where industrial waste is talking to the punctuation salesman these are the stiffest exclamation points ive ever seen industrial waste says

industrial can you deal with the salesman here while i interview this guy

sure

i take willie into the living room and brush the spiders off the furniture sit down i tell him do you have a resume

he reaches into his shirt pocket and takes out a folded sheet of paper which he hands me i unfold it and notice its handwritten that is to say handwritten is the least inaccurate word i can think of the sheet is covered with lines of tiny little squiggles that look like diagrams a biology student might make in his notes on bacteria tell me about yourself i say

well he says i used to run a phony talent agency i put ads in local papers and aspiring actors and

actresses and models and singers and such came
to me i charged them a whole lot of money to take
their pictures and then never did anything about
getting them jobs

how come youre not doing that any longer

i got tired of getting beaten up

after how many beatings

i didn't keep count

now i have to wonder here if this guy is really
smart enough or competent enough for me to want
to want to deal with him on the other hand the
fact that he tried a scam like that is a good sign he
has gumption no doubt i continue what did you do
after that

i worked at a resume service but i quit after a
few weeks talking to unemployed people all day
was too depressing

well i say i think youre the type of guy im looking for let me tell you what the deal is right now
im working two job theres the postal clerk job and
i also work for the cheep corporation

the cheep corporation i hear hiram cheep is the
richest man in the tri state area willie says so that
i can work the joke name into the story very oblig-
ing fellow what do you do there

i compare the signatures on all the canceled
paychecks to the employee signatures we have
on file to make sure the right person cashed them
now what i want to do is subcontract both jobs out
to people who will do them for minimum wage ill
still be clearing about a thousand dollars a week
for doing nothing later on i plan to look for a couple

more jobs and keep doing the same thing and i can rake in big piles of money while i stay at home working on my book its going to be a wonderful comprehensive work packed with insight

thats interesting willie says interrupting it sounds like a very exciting thing to be a part of id like the job

youre hired i say report to the main post office tomorrow morning and tell them youre working for me

we stand and shake hands i know a woman who might be interested in the cheep job willie says

good send her around sometime soon and ill talk to her

back in the dining room industrial waste and the punctuation salesman are on the floor picking up commas thunder the cat is darting about licking up what he can get i spilled some commas industrial says sheepishly

it occurs to me that the tails on the commas could injure thunder internally i pick him up and lock him in the bathroom so he cant get any more and then i call the vet and explain what happened

nothing to worry about the vet tells me they'll just pass through it might be slightly painful but it won't injure him

i get the vacuum cleaner out brush the spiders from it and rubber band an old handkerchief over the nozzle here i say ill get it i turn the vacuum on and sweep up the commas the handkerchief filters them so they dont go up the hose

hold the bag under them i tell the salesman he

picks up the bag shakes some spiders out of it and holds it under the vacuum nozzle i turn the vacuum off the commas fall into the bag ill take that bag i say and give me four more, and five bags of periods and four of quotation marks."

"how about upper case letters" the salesman asks.

"oh, yeah. that reminds me. question marks. one bag," i say.

"all right. and the upper case letters?"

"how much does the rest of this come to?"

the salesman plucks a spider off his calculator and flings the creature across the room. then he punches some numbers. "you have a tax and usage number?"

"no."

"then its sixty three dollars and thirty five cents. ill tell you what. since youve already bought this much, ill throw in a bag each of apostrophes and hyphens if you buy a carton of upper case letters."

"all right."

he punches some more numbers. "the grand total is eighty dollars and fifteen cents. i'll have to go out to the car for the carton."

i get my checkbook out, open it, shake a spider out, and begin writing the check. the punctuation salesman ducks out the side door.

the phone rings. i pick up the receiver, brush a spider off it, and answer. the caller is a swanky-looking dude dressed in black—never mind how i can tell over the phone—and he says, "this is death, and i'm sick of this shit."

"it doesn't have much impact," i tell him, "without the capital 'd.' if you want, you can hang on until the punctuation salesman comes back in with one, and then try again."

"all right."

the salesman comes back in. "here you go," he says, putting the carton of upper case letters on the table. "Here's my card. Call me anytime you need anything."

I look at the card:

THE YELLOW WAXY BUILDUP
PUNCTUATION CO.
Punctuation for all occasions
Mr. Transparent, Sales Consultant
Second Left Turn Off 3rd St. Past Main St. Ave.
555-2929

"Mr. Transparent," I say. "It's nice to meet you. If things work out all right with the punctuation I just bought, you'll have yourself a loyal customer."

"Yeah," Industrial says. "The guy he's been buying from is a real jerkface. And those quotation marks turned purple, remember?"

"How could I forget?" I say. "Talk about embarrassing."

"I've heard of that," Mr. Transparent says. "I can assure you, these quotation marks hold their blackness very well."

"And the question marks won't wilt?" Industrial asks.

Mr. Transparent smiles. "His question marks wilted?"

"Like a double cheeseburger on a whole wheat bagel with not enough mustard," Industrial says.

"Huh?"

"He's getting tired," I tell Mr. Transparent. "Thanks for dropping by. I have high hopes for your products."

"I'm sure you'll be well satisfied," he says. He shakes my hand with uncomfortable vigor and leaves.

An irate voice babbles indistinctly from the phone. Oh, gosh, I forgot all about Death. I pick up the phone.

"This is Death," he hisses. "And I'm sick of this shit."

"That's much better," say, and hang up.

The doorbell rings. "Can you get that?" I ask Industrial Waste. "I have to go to the bathroom."

"Sure," he says, and makes for the door.

In the bathroom, spiders are swimming around in the toilet. I suppose I don't have to get them out of the toilet to do what I have to do. Taken by surprise, they thrash around in the water.

In the living room, Industrial is sitting on the sofa with an attractive woman. I detect in her eyes a slightly twisted mentality.

"Hi," she says, jumping up perkily and offering her hand. "My name is Miffie McMillan. I've come about the job you're subcontracting out."

"Yes," I say. "I had two, but I hired a guy a few minutes ago. I forget which job he took; if you want to wait a minute, I can look back a few pages and see which one it was."

"All right."

"Okay, the one that's still open is the Cheep Corporation job. What you have to do is check the signatures on the canceled paychecks against the employee signatures we have on file to make sure the right person cashed them. How's that sound?"

"It sounds like a fascinating and challenging career."

"Do you have a resume?"

"No."

"Well, that's all right. Report to the seventh floor of the fabulous Cheep Building, the tallest building in the tri-state area, at nine o'clock Monday morning. Just tell them you're working for me."

"All right," she says, and bobs up again. "By the way, I can dance. Have you ever seen me dance?"

"I've only known you for about a page."

She does a turn and kicks. "See? Dancing. Would you pay me extra for dancing?"

"No."

Miffie leaves, and Industrial gives me a stack of envelopes. "The mail came," he says.

I shuffle through it. Mostly junk mail, ads for books. "How to subcontract your job out for fun and profit," one says. "How to deal with Death," another offers. "Are you getting the most for your punctuation dollar?" And "Fourteen reasons why 'The Air Conditioned Nightmare' should be your favorite song"

Hold on we're missing a period here

A pregnant pause

"Industrial," I say, "what happened to the periods?"

He looks down at his scrambled eggs, which are covered with black dots "You know," he says, "I didn't think this pepper tasted very peppery"

Soft White Underbelly, Part 3

I've had the hypnosis guy, Full Metal Thermostat—Metal—reporting back to me every month, apprising me of his progress as he works his way up the chain of command of...well, of whatever sort of sinister hierarchy we're dealing with. Day to day, he hasn't been consciously aware of anything out of the ordinary. He goes into his trance each time he makes contact with someone higher up, and he does his own hypnosis thing. He finds out who's at the next highest level, and so on. It's all very elegantly recursive.

When he reports back to me, knocking on my door triggers a post-hypnotic trance. I bring him in and sit him down, and he gives me the update. Each month, he's made his way one or two or three more steps up the ladder. Occasionally, he has something to report that's almost marginally interesting, but usually it's nothing except that the latest subject of hypnosis is merely receiving orders "from above" and is passing them on down.

Not one of these people seems to have a clue—or even the inclination to question—why so many levels of hierarchy are needed when very few of them are adding anything to the process except needless complexity. Oh, well. We'll never get the answer to that, anyway. The important thing is that we're close to finding out the...the ultimate goal of all this skullduggery.

Yes. And now, after a year, he has only the twenty-third—and last—level to tell me about. If everything has gone according to plan, he's reached the top, and it's time for the Big Payoff.

I have champagne in the refrigerator, ready for the celebration. And I'm sitting in the darkened living room by the window, watching through a narrow gap in the drapes, waiting for Full Metal Thermostat to show up. Just like the first time, my friends are hidden around the house. *So You Think You Can Perform a Root Canal* is playing on the teevee set.

Finally, Metal's car pulls up at the curb across the street. He sits for a few minutes, scoping out the house, and finally makes his approach. I move away from the window.

It's show time.

***

The knock on the door comes, and I answer. Metal goes into his trance. "Come in," I say.

He steps in and, as usual, sits down on the sofa. My friends come out from hiding.

"Did you make it to the top?" I ask.

"Yes, I did."

Industrial Waste gasps. The large, stuffed panda jumps up and down in excitement.

"What did you find out?"

"The world," he says, "is really run by the Illuminati. All the heads of state, the people we think are the leaders of the major world powers, have no idea of this. They're pawns, just like us, and they're hypnotized.

"Everything that happens in geopolitical politics is designed to control the masses, and it's been that way since the end of the Second World War."

"Holy smoke," Industrial says.

"The Cold War was nothing more or less than an elaborate charade to instill the fear of communism and nuclear war in the populace," Metal says. "That's what they use to exert control: fear. They fabricate a bad guy or some other sort of danger so the masses won't question the urgent, ultra-important need to have the government protect them. Then, those who are in control—the Illuminati—can do pretty much anything they want and get away with it because all the important stuff they want most to do can be explained under the guise of—yes, you guessed it—national security or public safety or somesuch. Very often—usually, in fact—the explanation makes such a complete mockery of logic and common sense that anyone with sufficient mental faculties to sit and listen to it should be horribly offended, but that doesn't matter. No matter how outrageous the lie is, very, very few people actually think about it, even for the tiniest instant. They simply accept it because they're scared.

"But there has never been any danger of nuclear war. There has never been more than a handful of nuclear weapons on the planet at any given time. A mere five or six. They set off one occasionally as a test detonation, just so people will know they have them."

"I don't believe· it," Collier Figg says. "What about all those thousands of bombs and missiles they have all over the world?"

"They don't exist. It would be silly to actually build enough to wipe out the human race, wouldn't it?"

"Uh, well, yeah," Collier says.

"The Cold War served its purpose very well. But it obviously wasn't going to last indefinitely. So even while it was still going on, they—those shadowy people in charge—began experimenting with other ways to instill fear.

"They tried out a number of different ideas. Crop circles—yes, that's what crop circles were supposed to be about. But they don't really inspire fear, do they?"

"Not so you'd notice," I say.

"No. The idea was that they were supposed to be all spooky and whatnot. But people got fascinated by them, and they became, actually, more of a joke than anything else. And disco music."

"Disco?" the large, stuffed panda says. "It was supposed to cause fear?"

"Yeah, disco was going to take over as the big threat to our way of life. *That* went nowhere."

"I wonder why..." Collier muses.

"But I *love* disco," the large, stuffed panda says.

"Now, it's global warming and the economy," Metal says.

"Global warming is fake?" Industrial says.

"The data is real, but the reporting is, shall we say, somewhat disingenuous."

"What about terrorism?"

"No, terrorism is real, through and through. There's no way to control it reliably, so it wouldn't be suitable for the purposes we're talking about here. See, they can control the economy with a fair degree of precision using a number of techniques. For example, they have extremely sophisticated software in the major stock exchanges. And those economic reports they issue all the time are fake as hell. Remember last month when they said 'the economy' lost a hundred thousand jobs?"

"No," the large, stuffed panda says.

"Well, it really gained a hundred and fifty thousand. Fake, fake, fake. But who was in a position to prove them wrong? Are you going to go out there personally and count all the unemployed people?"

"Not all by myself," Industrial says. "But if I had the proper funding and just the right people—"

"But if more people are working," I say, "wouldn't that have a positive effect on the economy?"

"A small one. But it would be more than offset by the negative effect of everyone believing employment is down. Economics is mostly a matter of human behavior, Thor. If you convince enough people that things are bad, even in a time of prosperity, things will sure enough get bad. And here's the scary part: the more drastic the change, the easier it is to accomplish."

"Okay, okay, I get the picture," I say. "But how do I fit into all this?"

"You're what they call an 'opinion leader.' If you believe something, you have a degree of influence over the people around you."

"He does not," Collier Figg says.

"Yes, he does, in regard to politics and current events and such. So, Thor, guys like me visit guys like you every month and hypnotize you and tell you what to think."

At first, no one is sure how to react.

Then my friends become outraged. "Rebellion!" Collier Figg shouts.

"Rebellion!" Industrial Waste shouts.

"Chicken intestines!" the large, stuffed panda shouts.

I shush them. This interrogation isn't finished yet, and the next question is the heaviest one of all: Who's the person at the very top level? But merely thinking about it scares me. This is the biggest of big-time stuff, and maybe I'm better off not knowing. Plausible deniability, and all that.

Even so, a pretty good idea takes shape in my head: I still have the young lover's gun. I take it off the mantelpiece, check to make sure it's loaded, and give it to Full Metal Thermostat. "Go find the person in charge of all this and blow his brains out," I tell him. "And make it messy. Very messy."

He looks the gun over carefully, as if appraising its value, and leaves.

"Do you think that'll take care of the problem?" Industrial asks.

"I don't know," I say. I'm not even sure exactly what "the problem" is. It occurs to me to wonder, though, how all the stuff we just learned will affect Stanley Dirndl's petition for a Better America. Or maybe the question is merely how it *would have affected* it, now that the stuff we just learned is soon going to be inoperative. Or something. Or maybe it won't. The machinations behind such a plot must be extensive beyond comprehension. Maybe this campaign of instilling fear will continue indefinitely, no matter what happens to any individual, simply because of inertia.

Ah, but then again, the buck has to stop somewhere, doesn't it?

Ah, but then yet again, I could find out easily enough. This would certainly change the vision of the future hidden away in that yard-sale cello case, right? Whatever horrible, bleak image that currently resides in that case, the picture that stops angry dogs in their tracks and turns adults into catatonic puddles of scared-witless goo—that image would surely change into a bright, cheerful picture of sunshine and puppies and picnics in the park.

Pffft...I'm not going to look. No way. Maybe it would only change it into something marginally less nightmarish.

All I know is this: If a guy has an opportunity

to improve the world, doesn't he have to give it a shot? Doesn't he have an obligation?

Ah, but then yet one more time *again*, what the hell am I thinking about?

I undergo a moment of panic. Will this mess everything up? Should I run after Metal and call off the hit?

No. No need for that. If we get rid of the person who's behind the whole "control the populace with fear" scheme, it should increase the chances that Stanley's petition will be approved!

Yes, yes. I'm only glad that I was able to play a role in helping usher in the Age of the Better America.

***

Later, the guys are gone. I begin cleaning up, feeling pleased with myself. I've successfully overthrown the people who rule the world, and without leaving my living room—oh, how long I've waited to say that!

I open the hall closet to get the vacuum out, and a body with a running chainsaw sticking out of its back falls out. God, I hate when that happens.

The doorbell rings. I turn the chainsaw off and answer the door. It's a guy in a football jersey. He has a case of beer under one arm and some video tapes in his other hand.

"Hi," he says. "You by yourself?"

"Yes," I answer through clenched teeth.

"I'm the married guy secrets guy. I come over

sometime shortly after guys get married, and we sit around watching sports on TV—I have these tapes because nothing but golf is on today. We sit around watching sports and guzzling beer, and I tell you secrets about how to be a married guy."

It would seem he has the wrong house. But then again, he has a case of beer. "Come on in," I tell him. "The wife is going to be gone all day."

Solitaire America, Part 2

"We begin tonight with the inspirational story of Plausibleville resident Stanley Dirndl, who lost two great, well-paying jobs in a span of less than six months. But rather than sit around whining and complaining about it, Stanley decided to do something. And what he did will have a profound effect on society down through the ages. Samantha Poochley has the story."

"Thank you, Tim. I'm reporting from Plausibleville, where Stanley Dirndl, faced with the prospect of living the rest of his life as an unemployed loser, decided to take action and work for the betterment of America. Stanley, what did you do?"

"I circulated a petition to request that the government make America better."

"How did you get started with that?"

"It's not easy, lemme tell you. Do you know how much paperwork is involved in getting a permit to circulate a petition?"

"What do you have to do?"

"You have to submit the text of your petition,

describe the current situation and why it should be changed, explain what you think should be done, and why and how it would it would be an improvement, disclose the geographic area where the petition will be circulated—including detailed demographics with age, income, and height/weight statistics of your target area. You have to include photographs and sound recordings of the affected area. You have to include notarized statements from at least eight attorneys and eight doctors. You have to conduct economic, environmental, moral, and spiritual impact studies. You have to explain why you're qualified to have a credible opinion on the matter. Then they give you five different lie detector tests.

"After that, you have to write book reviews of your ten favorite science fiction novels and fill out a five-hundred page questionnaire asking about your opinions on various household cleaners. They make you undergo a physical examination, during which they measure the length of every hair on your body and make you up to look like Woody Woodpecker. Then you have to have to prepare lunch for everyone on the city council every day for a month."

"That sounds like a lot of work."

"Sure. Only the most dedicated petitioners get through it."

"But you persevered, Stanley."

"Yes, I did. And after all that, I still had to circulate the petition. That was the really hard part."

"How so?"

"Lots of people resisted. They were suspicious. They called me a communist. They called me a terrorist. They called me funny looking. They ridiculed me. They punched me in the ear. They gave me wedgies and swirlies. They threw bloody pig hearts at me."

"But you got the signatures."

"Yes, I did. Eventually."

"And then what happened?"

"I had to fill out thousands more pages of paperwork to process the petition. At this point, I began to suspect the whole thing was just to discourage people from circulating petitions. But this was *important*, Samantha."

"Yes, it was."

"I refused to give up."

"So after you got the signatures and had the petition processed, what happened?"

"A few weeks later, I received a letter. They granted the request, and now we're going to get a better America."

"When does it go into effect?"

"On June twelfth. When you wake up that morning, everything should be better."

"I think we're all looking forward to that. A better America, and it's all due to your heroic efforts. Every citizen owes you an enthusiastic thank-you, Stanley."

"I didn't do it for the glory. I did it because someone had to."

"Wow," Industrial Waste says. "A better America."

"Awesome," I say, popping open another beer.

"I think we're all looking forward to a better America, thanks to Stanley Dirndl. This is Samantha Poochley reporting from Plausibleville."

"Thank you, Samantha. In other news, two men were apprehended at the Cook County tax assessor's office after a high-speed chase..."

Just the Right People

"Supper's ready," I tell Industrial Waste.

"Quiet. I'm trying to do something." He leans in closer to his computer monitor and pounds on the keyboard a little harder. It's hard for me to imagine that he has something to do that's more important than eating supper while it's still hot, but... well, whatever. I'm not his mother. (Of course, his mother calls me two or three times a day to ask whether he's staying warm and eating the proper number of servings from all the major food groups. I always tell her yes, no matter what he's doing. I assured her he was eating properly all through his six-week binge of living on nothing but pink cotton candy. I thought it might worry her, and there's no sense in that.)

I go to the kitchen and plate up one of the pterodactyl steaks from the skillet. I hope Industrial wraps up whatever he's doing soon; pterodactyl meat really isn't very good if you let it sit more than a few minutes.

Just as I'm finishing my steak, Industrial comes into the room. "What do you have there?" he asks. "Smells delicious."

"Pterodactyl steaks."

"What's the occasion?"

"No occasion. I just decided I deserved it because I'm me."

"Yeah, boy!" Industrial gets a plate from the cabinet and takes the other steak. "I'm gonna do me some eatin'!" He sits down, picks up the steak with his hands, and bites in. But it takes great effort for him to bite into it. He pulls and pulls and pulls, grunting and squinting all the while, with his face turning red and tears welling up in his eyes. He finally gives up and flops the steak down. He's breathing heavily. "I hope you didn't pay much for these things. I hope you didn't pay *anything*."

"Dude, you let it sit too long. I called you to supper twenty minutes ago."

He sighs. "Oh, well."

"What were you doing in there, anyway?"

"Planning my new project. What with all this stuff going on about Stanley Dirndl and his petition for a Better America, I was inspired to do something monumental. I'm going to take inventory of everything on the planet."

"That sounds terribly time consuming," I say.

"I suppose so. But then again, I have a lot of time on my hands."

I think about it for a bit: An inventory of everything on the planet. It could be handy to have info like that. Who wouldn't want to know how many coffee cans there are? How many copies of

The Book of the Damned? How many ocarinas? I'm getting unbearably curious just thinking about it. "How are you going to pay for it?" I ask.

"Government grant. I'm going to hire people, give each one a laptop computer and a half-dozen official Worldwide Inventory T-shirts, and pay 'em five dollars an hour."

"All over the world?"

"Well, yeah, Thor. It's kinda gonna be necessary to have people all over the world."

"Have you applied for the grant?"

"Applied and received. I have a big, fat bank account and a checkbook full of fresh, new, virginal checks waiting for me to make whatever payments I have to make. What I was doing on the computer a few minutes ago...I was writing a help-wanted ad I'm going to post on Gregslist."

"To hire inventory takers?"

"Yes, exactly. But I have to be careful. This is a deceptively complex project, and it requires very specific, advanced skills. I need to make sure I hire just the right people."

"Sure."

"I need highly competent experts. World-class intellects."

"I can understand that. It's a big job."

"I mean, I hate to say it, Thor, but, well...like, for example, I don't think you would qualify."

I'm relieved. I don't think I would want to go around knocking on people's doors asking to see every item in the house.

"Let's face it, Thor, you just don't have what it

takes. I'm sure you have a good work ethic, but I'm talking about *skills*. If I'm going to be honest, you really do fall short in that department. I'm sorry."

"Too bad for me," I say.

"Yeah, I know. I love you dearly, Thor—in a strictly straight-guy, heterosexual, brotherly type of way, that is—but I think we both have to face up to your shortcomings. You're simply not suited for this inventory."

I think back over the last few minutes, trying to remember everything we said since Industrial came into the room. I'm pretty sure I didn't ask for a job. "Well," I say, trying to stanch the flow of Industrial's ongoing—and rather enthusiastic, it would seem, as well as arbitrary and completely unnecessary—rejection, "I guess I'll have to look elsewhere for a job."

"Yeah. I'm sorry."

"Don't worry. You said it yourself: You need just the right people."

"I'm glad you understand."

"Oh, sure. Have you hired anyone yet?"

He smiles sheepishly. "Do you really want to know?"

"You hired Collier Figg."

"And the large, stuffed panda. They're going to be regional managers."

"Of what?"

"Regions, Thor. Of regions."

Well, at least he didn't hire Chickenfeet. That would be too much.

"And I might hire Chickenfeet."

"Oh, come on. What on earth could Chickenfeet possibly do to contribute?" I don't particularly care that he doesn't want me...but not wanting me, coupled with wanting Chickenfeet...I'm not sure I like the implication.

"He can do stuff. He has...enthusiasm."

"He has stupidity." So do Collier Figg and the large, stuffed panda, but not quite as much.

"Don't be a hater, Thor. It's unseemly. Besides, it's not a done deal. Not yet. We're still negotiating over what kind of car he's going to get."

"Car?"

"You have to understand, a Jaguar is great. But it's not the right kind of car for work like this." He gets up and opens the refrigerator. "Now, since you fucked up those steaks, I have to find something else to eat. Do we have any beans?"

***

Industrial has called a meeting. And of course, he's doing it at my house so as to rub it in my face that I'm not included. I mean, no, he didn't come right out and say it, but I know the score.

It was supposed to start twenty minutes ago, and Chickenfeet is just now the first person to show up. Industrial called to say he's late because he's stopping to get beer, and I suppose Collier Figg and the large, stuffed panda are being fashionably late—that is to say, if you can assume anything about those two could be described as fashionable.

Chickenfeet wants me to see the company car

he has for the inventory job, so I'm standing in front of the house pretending to admire his 1977 Chevette. It's his first car, and he told me that last night, he spent five hours driving around the block where he lives, pretending to be in the Indianapolis 500. "The speed limit's twenty-five," he says. "So it was kinda lame. I mean, like lame for a world-famous race. But still, I had to do it."

"Anyone would," I say.

He unloads several cases of beer onto a small hand truck and wheels it into the house. "This job could be a big opportunity for me," he says. "We're going to have to knock on doors and ask people whether we can count the stuff in their homes. Do you know what kinds of people we'll be dealing with?"

"No, I don't," I say. I don't want to talk about this. I wish the others would show up.

"All kinds. The rich and the poor. The young and the old. The tall and the short. The famous and the useless. And that includes hot chicks, too. Industrial promised me I would meet lots and lots of hot chicks."

"Sounds good," I say. But Industrial would have said anything he thought Chickenfeet might want to hear. *Hot chicks? Yeah, man. More than you can imagine.* As for me, I'm doubtful that Chickenfeet has the know-how or the...the *style*, if you want to call it that, to capitalize on any...er...carnal opportunities. He's cool to hang out with, but really, he's a dork.

"It's going to be the beginning of a whole new

life for me," Chickenfeet says.

"A whole new life," I echo.

***

Eventually, Collier Figg shows up. He has a small hand truck with cases of beer stacked on it. "I brought beer," he says.

"I'm going to meet lots of hot chicks," Chickenfeet says.

"You and me both, buddy," Collier says. He breaks open one of the cases. He pulls out a couple of cans and tosses one to Chickenfeet. To me, he says, "Sorry, bud. This beer is for Worldwide Inventory staff only."

"That's all right," I say.

"I'd really like to give you one, but I can't."

"No worries. Really."

"Glad you understand."

A few minutes later, the large, stuffed panda arrives. He also has a small hand truck with cases of beer stacked on it. He high-fives Collier and Chickenfeet. "Hot chicks, hot chicks," they chant. Collier hands the large, stuffed panda a beer.

"Did Industrial promise all you guys hot chicks?"

"Well," the large, stuffed panda says, "it kinda stands to reason, doesn't it? We're bound to run into some while we're out in the field. Hot chicks always think stuffed animals are cute." He pauses and then adds, "*All* of them."

An idea occurs to me. "Industrial told you that?"

"Yeah. He's been around. He knows."

"And how much is he paying you?" I ask.

"Huh?" Chickenfeet says.

"How much is he paying you?"

"He bought us cars," Collier says.

"1977 Chevettes?"

"How did you know?"

"That's what Chickenfeet got."

"It's a fun car," Chickenfeet says.

"I'm sure it is. But you haven't answered my question. How much is he paying you?"

Collier looks at Chickenfeet. Chickenfeet looks at the large, stuffed panda. The large, stuffed panda is looking out the window. He's gazing very intently at something off in the distance. "Is that a helicopter or a bird?" he finally says, pointing.

"It's a communications satellite," I say without looking.

"Oh, yeah."

"So he's not actually paying you anything."

Collier looks at Chickenfeet. Chickenfeet looks at the large, stuffed panda. "I don't think it's a satellite," the large, stuffed panda says.

"But the babes," Chickenfeet says.

"Yeah, the babes," Collier says. "Hot ones."

"Lots of 'em. More than we can count."

This leads me to wonder how high these guys can count—which in turn leads me to doubt their qualifications for the job.

"Actually, I think it's a small cloud that someone spray painted gray," the large, stuffed panda says.

"What is a hot babe going to do with some dorky guy who comes knocking on her door asking to count her stuff?" I ask.

"Thor, if you have to ask..." Chickenfeet says.

"Are you saying Industrial is taking advantage of us?" Collier says.

"You have to reach your own conclusion about that," I say. "But, you know, I think you should consider that a paycheck is normally the primary way people are compensated for work, as opposed to old cars and promises of sex that are so vague as to be meaningless."

"I think you're just resentful that he wouldn't hire you," Chickenfeet says.

"Sort of a bluish-gray," the large, stuffed panda says.

"You haven't gotten laid lately, have you?" Collier says.

"Industrial Waste didn't promise me I would," I say.

"And we get the computers," Collier says. "The laptops."

"Yeah," Chickenfeet says. "The computers."

"Can I see one?"

Chickenfeet reaches down and opens his backpack. He takes out a bulky, square-ish case, lays it on the coffee table, and flips the clasps open. "Are you ready for this?" he says.

"Ready whenever you are," I say.

He opens the case, and we look. Chickenfeet grins smugly. Collier looks on in approval.

I move around to get a better view. "This is a

typewriter," I say. "It's not even an electric model. It's an old manual typewriter. Probably made around 1960, by the looks of it."

"A typewriter?" Collier says.

"I've heard of those," Chickenfeet says.

"I wonder how you get up high enough to spray paint a cloud," the large, stuffed panda says. His voice is very dreamy-like-sounding.

"I wondered where the screen was," Collier says.

"I mean, if you go up in a helicopter, the blades would blow the cloud away, wouldn't they?"

"I tried to search for Asian robot cowgirl porn, but it didn't give me any results at all," Collier said.

"Don't you think the facts speak for themselves?" I ask.

"Well..." Chickenfeet says.

"You shouldn't be searching for porn on company computers," Industrial says.

"And say you pull up in front of some hot babe's house in a 1977 Chevette. Is that going to impress her?"

"It might," Chickenfeet says stubbornly.

"Is it? *Really?*"

"Well, I'll admit that mine has a few scratches," Collier says.

"And mine has that huge dent in the fender that shreds my tire with jagged metal when I try to turn left," Chickenfeet says.

"You have tires on yours?" Collier says.

"I suppose they could use a big, huge ladder to

get up there, but what would they lean it against?"
the large, stuffed panda says. It's clear that he's
thinking really hard about this.

"You know, you might be right. He might just
be taking advantage of us," Collier says.

Chickenfeet nudges the large, stuffed panda.
"What do you think?"

"Huh?" the large, stuffed panda says.

"What do you think?" Chickenfeet asks me.

"As I said, you have to reach your own conclusion."

***

We turn on a Benny the Bouncer DVD and watch
in silence, waiting for Industrial to come home. I
assume the others are stewing and fretting, giving their position careful consideration, thinking
about how to confront him.

Finally, after about a half hour, Industrial
shows up with two hand trucks loaded with cases
of beer. "Hey, guys," he says. "I have beer."

"Beer!" the large, stuffed panda says. He jumps
up and down in excitement.

"Yeah, beer. But Thor, I'm sorry. None for you.
This is only for inventory staff."

"Fine with me," I say.

"I hate to have to draw the line this way," he
says. "But really, it's for the best."

"I understand."

"You know I'm not excluding you just to be
mean."

"I get it."

"I'm not a mean person."

"I don't think you are."

"If only you had what it takes to be a Worldwide Inventory worker, it would be different."

And then I utter a sentence I never would have expected to issue forth from my mouth: "I don't need beer," I say.

Industrial smiles condescendingly and pats me on the shoulder. "I think it's possible that we could have a place for you in the organization if you want to apply again, say, in about five years. I'm willing to bet that by then, you'll have *developed* enough to serve some sort of *menial* but marginally useful purpose in the organization."

"I'll keep it in mind."

Industrial rips open one of his cases of beer and passes cans around to the others. The large, stuffed panda drops his, picks it up, and pops the tab. Beer spews all over him. "Hey!" he cries.

"Industrial," Collier Figg says, "are you taking advantage of us?"

"Yeah," Chickenfeet says. "Are you?"

"Huh?"

"Don't 'huh' me, buddy-boy," Collier says. "Don't think we haven't noticed that you're not paying us."

"But the babes, the cars, the computers," Industrial says.

"Yeah," Chickenfeet says. "I forgot about that. The babes..." His eyes take on a faraway look.

"Hot babes," Industrial says. "Smokin' hot!"

The large, stuffed panda starts jumping up and down. "Hot babes!" he shouts.

Collier frowns. "Wait a minute," he says, a low growl in his voice. "We're talking about paychecks—which, as I'm trying to point out, have been left out of the deal for some reason."

"But the babes..." Industrial insists.

"How do you expect us to score with the babes if we're not getting paid?" Collier says. "How are we going to buy stylish clothes to impress them? How are we going to take them to dinner?"

The faraway look in Chickenfeet's eyes goes away. Suddenly, he's right here with us. "And no computers," he says. "Those things are really..." He turns to me. "What did you call those things?"

"Typewriters."

"Yeah, typewriters. Those things are really typewriters. You can't even get the Internet on them. Did you know that?"

The large, stuffed panda looks around. "Is that right? Then what are they good for?"

"I'm not sure," Chickenfeet says.

"Who knows?" Collier says. "But the real problem here is that this guy..." and here he jabs at the air toward Industrial, "has been trying to take advantage of us."

"I say we quit," Chickenfeet says.

"Now wait a minute," Industrial says. "Let's not do anything rash."

"I'm going home," Collier says. "*Bowling for Penicillin* starts in fifteen minutes, and Pindy is going for her fifth win in a row."

Chickenfeet's eyes widen. "Really? Pindy's winning streak is still going?"

"Oh, yeah. Didn't you see it last week? She staged an amazing come-from-behind win." He gets up and makes his way to the door.

"If you're quitting, I want the cars back," Industrial says.

Collier stops and turns around. "If you insist on getting the cars back, we're going to shove them up your nose."

"We'll do it, too," the large, stuffed panda says. "Don't think we won't." He gets up and joins Collier at the door. After a moment, Chickenfeet catches on and gets up, too.

"C'mon, I need you guys," Industrial says. "I'll start paying you. I promise."

"Too late now," Collier says. "You've already proven that we can't trust you." He leads Chickenfeet and the large, stuffed panda out. A moment later, three noisy engines start. I look out the window and see huge clouds of black smoke billowing out of their cars. Amid much rattling and clattering, they drive away in a sort of small clunker parade.

"Well, that's that," I say.

"What am I going to do now?" Industrial says. "Thor, I need your help."

"How so?"

"My people just walked out on me."

"But the problem is, I'm not up to the task. I don't have what it takes."

A pained expression washes over Industrial's

face. "Oh, *that*," he says. "See, that was just a bar-
gaining tactic. I was going to offer you a job, and a
good one, too. All that stuff was laying the groundwork for negotiating your price."

"Groundwork."

"Yeah, all the best negotiators do it." He reaches into an open case of beer and pulls out a can.
"Look, man. Here's a beer. You can have it."

"Don't try to give me a beer. You and I both
know it'll take me five years to develop far enough
to do the most menial job in your project. You said
so yourself."

"Aw, c'mon, man. Don't be a hardass. I'm in
need here."

"That's not my problem."

Industrial puts the beer down. "Thor, if I don't
get this inventory project going, I'm going to have
to pay back the grant."

"So? Pay it back. It doesn't look to me as if
you've spent very much of it."

"Thor, that's the problem. I've spent almost all
of it. Why do you think I couldn't pay the guys?"

"You mean the grant was only enough to buy
some old Chevettes and typewriters?"

"Oh, it was much bigger. It was ten million
dollars. But..." Industrial trails off. He squirms
around uncomfortably. There's something he
doesn't want to tell me.

"You spent it on something stupid, didn't you?"

"No."

"Yes, you did."

"It wasn't stupid. It was a good deal. A *great*

deal."

"What was?"

He heaves a sigh. "Ice cream."

I start to say something but stop myself. I have to think about this. "You mean you bought ten million dollars worth of ice cream?"

"No, of course not." He looks at me as if I'm an idiot. Maybe I am.

"But you just said—"

"I said it was a great deal. I got *twenty* million dollars worth of ice cream for ten million."

"I see."

"Well, not actually ten million. More like nine point ninety-nine million. I kept a little of it back to pay for the stuff I bought for the guys. You might as well say ten, though."

"So why don't you sell it?"

"Well, that's the problem. I kinda sorta can't."

I think I'm catching on. "Where is this ice cream?"

"Thor, why are you asking so many questions?"

"Why won't you answer?"

"Okay, okay. It's gone. It melted. I put it in storage, and it melted. There's no ice cream left."

"Just to make sure I understand: You put it in regular storage? The same type of storage unit you would use for, like, furniture or whatever?"

"Yeah."

"Why didn't you rent some sort of industrial freezer facility?"

"Thor, do you know how expensive that would be?"

"And so now, you expect me to help you take inventory of everything on the planet, for free, even though you've made it excessively clear that I'm not qualified, because you let ten million dollars worth of ice cream melt?"

"Twenty million, but it was an accident. And not for free. I have enough left to buy another Chevette. Thor, do you want me to buy you a Chevette?"

"I'm going to bed."

"Wait. I have another idea. Are you still looking for someone to subcontract that job you have at the Cheep Corporation? I could earn the money to pay it back."

"Well, gee, Industrial. This is kind of awkward. I hate to tell you this, but I need just the right person. I'm not sure you're qualified. I don't think you have what it takes."

"Oh, Thor. That's petty. I'm disappointed that you would do this to me."

"Ask me again five years from now. Maybe you'll develop far enough to be able to do something menial for me."

"Thor, please."

"You're not going to make ten million dollars doing that job, anyway."

"Yeah, well, right. I guess you have a point. Besides, I'd rather avoid having to work."

***

Now, a week later, Industrial is in his room,

furiously typing on his computer. I hear the click-clack of the keys as I lie on my bed reading. It's not loud; it doesn't disturb me. But it gets me curious.

I go to his room and knock on the door.

"Yeah?" he says.

I crack the door open. "Industrial, what are you doing?"

"Working on my inventory project."

"I thought it fell through."

"Yeah, but still, I'm on the hook for ten million dollars. I have to produce some kind of results."

I walk over and look at his computer screen. He has a spreadsheet open, with columns of words and numbers:

Almonds	3,475,927,645
Ambulances	5,689,227
Amphetamines	10,498,153,662
Ampoules	124,821,853,111

And so on. "You're going to tell them you've been counting almonds?" I ask.

"Not counting. Weighing. Stuff like that, I measure in ounces."

"I see."

"Yeah. That's the only way to do it. But...do you think this number looks all right? Is it realistic? I have no idea. I'm just pulling numbers out of my butt. Do you think there are more almonds in the world?"

"I don't know," I say. "I don't expect they would try to verify your numbers, though."

Industrial grins. "Yeah. I hadn't thought of that."

I peer at the spreadsheet. Something's missing. "Where are amoebas?"

He looks up at me, incredulous. "I'm not going to count amoebas, Thor. That would be *silly*."

Who Let Him in Here?

"My landlord," Collier Figg says, "is a Nazi war criminal." He stubs out his cigarette and looks down at his left foot.

We're playing cards, Collier and I, with Charles Fort and the large, stuffed panda. Throughout the game, reality has been putting on a nice, semi-entertaining sideshow for us. The face cards turned into Peanuts cartoons and then to pictures of Andy Rooney in provocative poses and then to display ads from the New Orleans Yellow Pages. The table itself turned into a tree stump. Cloudy-looking stuff appeared near the ceiling and rained wheat pennies on us. Later, the cloud formed itself into a tiny fifteenth-century Chinese army. It was picturesque to look at but terribly loud.

This is the last damn time I'm going to play cards with Charles Fort.

"I have it all figured out," Collier's saying.

"Yeah? How so?" I ask—and let it be said that I don't want to ask, but I know Collier won't let it go until he gets to explain.

"For one thing, he's an old German guy," Collier

says.

"There are millions of old German guys," I say.

"Yes! And old German guys are the only people who could possibly be Nazi war criminals."

"I've seen your landlord," I say. "He's pretty old, but I don't think he's old enough. I mean, that was a long time ago."

"Details," Collier says impatiently. "Mere details."

My stack of *Writer's Digest* magazines in the corner spontaneously combusts. "You're hypnotized!" Fort shouts at me. "The astronomers have you hypnotized, and you don't even know it! You fool!"

This is an affront, and I'm taken aback. Collier regards Fort for a moment. "Chill out," he says—Collier, that is—and then, to me, continues. "And his name is Bill Hershey. What do you think of that?"

"Makes me think of chocolate," I say. Don Ho strolls in from the kitchen with a beer in his hand. He smiles sheepishly and leaves.

"It's not a German name," Collier goes on. "Why wouldn't a German guy have a German name? Because he changed it, that's why. And why would he change it?"

"Do any of us know what a German name is?" Fort hisses. He leans across the table toward Collier. "Every breath you take contains a molecule from Julius Caesar's last breath."

Collier recoils. "That's morbid!"

"And here you are worrying about Nazi war

criminals and lumps in the continuum of existence," Fort says.

"Lumps?"

"As if anyone truly were, or truly weren't, a Nazi war criminal, or even German, for that matter." Fort sits back and lays his hands over his belly, looking like Uncle Ned after he's finished stuffing himself at Thanksgiving dinner. "I would advise you, my friend, to look beyond the tip of your nose."

"Who let him in here?" the large, stuffed panda says.

"I'm going to get another beer," I say. As I push my chair back, it hits something solid—a palm tree is growing from the floor behind me. I squeeze out. "Anybody else want one?"

No one does. I go into the kitchen and take a beer from the refrigerator, open it, and guzzle. Nazi war criminal, for God's sake. How many of those guys could possibly be left? And more pressing, where's my fingernail clipper? I have a hangnail that's bothering the living fuck out of me.

I finish the beer, get another, and go back to the game. Fort's dealing. "All right," he says. "This is Madagascar high-low crash trump poker. I deal everyone two cards face-up, like this. Then each player gets to pick a card from the player to his left, and that card is exchanged with a new card from the deck. The new cards from the deck are dealt face-up. Then the old cards are turned face down, and since we have only four players, we add another card from the deck to make a dummy hand

in the middle of the table. Any player who can't
beat the dummy hand must fold immediately."

"I'm getting bored," the large, stuffed panda
says. "Why don't you come up with a new one?"

Fort raises his hand, as if to wag his finger in
the large, stuffed panda's face and scold him, but
Collier interrupts. "And another thing," he says.
"He's been going out every Friday night for the last
two months. Guess who meets on Friday nights?"

"The local chapter of the American Nazi Party," a woman's voice says.

"What's going on?" Collier looked around, confused. "There aren't supposed to be any women at
a poker game unless they're putting sandwiches
on the table and leaving immediately. Did one of
you guys turn into a woman?"

"Amelia Earhart," the voice says. "Don't you
remember?" Yes, yes, of course. She was at Waterhead's bachelor party, jumping out of a cake. Fun
times, even if we couldn't see her because her body
is in another dimension. Her voice seems to be
coming from the empty space to Fort's left, in front
of the stream of pennies raining from the ceiling.

"Yes," Collier says. "That's who meets on Friday nights."

"Are you certain that's where he goes?" Amelia
asks.

"No, but I plan to find out this week. I'm going
to follow him. Do you want to come with me?"

"I wouldn't go to a hospital with you if both my
legs got cut off," Fort says.

"That can be arranged," Collier says.

"You don't have any evidence," I say. "Not one, single, solitary iota of a hint of a shred of evidence."

"That's why I need to follow him Friday night," Collier says, as if explaining to a child. "What would you say if we followed him, and he went to the headquarters of the American Nazi Party?"

"What do you expect?" I ask. "Do you think he's going to lead us to a building that has a sign out front that says, 'Local Chapter of the American Nazi Party—Public Welcome'?" A dozen three-foot-tall carrots with arms and legs dance across the room in a ragged formation. Fort takes a small notebook from his shirt pocket and begins writing.

"Well..." Collier obviously wants desperately to cling to this idea.

"Look it up in the phone book. I'll bet they're not even listed."

"What do you think?" Collier challenges. "That it's illegal? Because it's not."

Suddenly I'm not so sure. It just seems to me like something the members would want to keep on the downlow, in the shadowy corners of the out-skirts of society. But what do I know? "The point is," I say, "even if he goes to this Nazi meeting, it's probably going to be at somebody's house, or in the basement of some musty old bookstore or some-thing. How are we going to know what's going on inside?"

"Oh, come on. Pull your head out of the sand, Thor." That doesn't answer my question, but it would be useless to pursue it.

"How do you know the Nazi Party meets on

Fridays?" Amelia asks.

Collier rolls his eyes. "You people are unbelievable. The Internet. How else?"

How else? Indeed.

"Look," Collier says, "the only way we have even the slightest chance of finding out is to follow him. Sure, we might not get anywhere with it, but don't we have to try?"

The ceiling turns to wax and sags in the middle. I give Fort a dirty look. He smiles sheepishly and continues writing.

"So what if he does go to this meeting?" the large, stuffed panda asks. "Does that make him a war criminal?"

Collier looks as if he's being strangled. "Do you want to go or not? I need the help, but with or without anybody else, I have to go."

"Count me in," I tell him. He needs someone there who has more sense than he does. Even if it's me.

"I'd like to go," the large, stuffed panda says.

"I'd be delighted to have you along," Collier says pleasantly.

"What about me?" Amelia asks.

"You, too."

Fort sits back and adjusts his tie. His beard falls off. Without it, he looks twenty years younger.

***

We meet at Collier's apartment Friday afternoon. I'm the first to arrive. "Now, we're only going to follow him," I say. "We're not going to cause any trouble. Under no circumstances will we cause trouble. Right?"

"Of course."

I'm not convinced. But, of course, the reason I'm coming along is to prevent the trouble that I'm sure he'll try to brew up.

Amelia arrives next, and the large, stuffed panda a couple minutes later. Collier's landlord lives next door—this is a neighborhood of huge, old Victorian houses that have been chopped up into apartments, and Mr. Hershey owns most of the block. "Slumlord," Collier calls him, but the area's actually rather nice—in spite of having Collier as a resident.

And now, Collier sits by the window watching for his landlord to leave. The rest of us sit around watching TV. The news is on, and there's a story about a guy who danced the Charleston while making his way down the length of a shopping mall. Who could imagine such a thing?

Shortly after seven, Collier calls us to the window. "There he is," he tells us, pointing. A thin, wrinkled old man slowly makes his way from the house next door to a Chevy parked at the curb. "Remember what he looks like. You'll probably have to testify in court."

That remark causes me to worry, just a little bit, that maybe Collier has some sort of cockamamie scheme that'll be worse than whatever I might have expected. I can't say anything, though, because it would cause a horrible argument. I'll just have to be vigilant tonight.

We watch as Mr. Hershey gets into his car and starts it. As soon as he pulls away from the curb, we rush out to Collier's car and pile in. "This is it," Collier says, his voice trembling. He starts up and pulls out behind his landlord.

As far as I can tell, Mr. Hershey doesn't suspect anything. He takes us halfway across town, eventually pulling into the parking lot at Victor Frankenstein High School. The place is crowded; there's a football game—Frankenstein vs. Sancho Panza Memorial High School. "Do you think this is the Nazi meeting?" I say, dosing my voice up with extra amounts of sarcastic acid because I know subtlety will be lost on Collier. "There sure are a lot of them."

"No," he says. "He's onto us. He's just trying to throw us off. Keep your eye on him."

Mr. Hershey parks and gets out of the car. He falls in with the crowd walking around the school building toward the football field. It's been years since I last went to a high school football game; I'd forgotten what it was like. The kids are in very high spirits. There's a constant din of hollering and cheering, and boys are hitting on girls and trying to sneak liquor in. Girls are standing around in clumps, talking. Parents and teachers socialize. Cops thread their way through the crowd, making sure their presence is known.

"Hmmm..." Collier says. He swings into the parking space the security guard is waving him into. We get out and follow the crowd. Mr. Hershey's about fifty feet ahead of us. We're able to keep him in sight intermittently at that distance. He gets in line at the ticket booth.

"He's really going to the game," Industrial says.

Collier snorts. "We'll see about that. He'll give us the slip first chance he gets, and then he'll be out of here, going off to his meeting."

"He knows we're following?" the large, stuffed panda says.

"I doubt it. He would probably assume someone's following, though. That's the way you have to operate when you're doing stuff like the stuff he's doing."

"What's he doing?" the large, stuffed panda asks. "I'm still not clear about that."

Collier shoots him a contemptuous look, and we get in line. About a dozen people are between Mr. Hershey and us. "Amelia," Collier says, "are you here?"

"Yes."

Collier looks around. "Where?"

"Here." The voice is coming from somewhere to my right, which is just in front of Collier.

"Huh?" He turns to me. "Thor, is Amelia here?"

"You heard her, didn't you?"

"I'm telling the truth," she says.

"Yeah, okay," Collier says. "Why don't you hang around up there and keep an eye on him?"

"Okay."

Two kids behind us start snickering. "Where'd you get your friend here," one says, nudging the large, stuffed panda. "Did you win him at the carnival?"

"Hey, be cool," Collier says.

"Aw, he's taking up for his friend," the other kid says. "Hey, Roly-Poly, you have a good friend here."

"I know," the large, stuffed panda says. "A couple years ago he let me borrow some of his Alice Cooper CDs. Did you know Alice Cooper is really a man? What were his parents thinking?"

"I wonder how far he'd roll," the first kid says. And before we realize what's happening, the kids have pushed the large, stuffed panda over and given him a hefty shove.

The school building is downhill—rather steepish-ly so, in fact—from the football field. So the large, stuffed panda goes rolling down, arms and legs flailing. "Help!" he screams. Other folks look at him and point and laugh. He continues rolling, picking up speed, and caroms off a bench at the edge of a small garden. He goes airborne and crashes through a large window in the cafeteria.

"Holy crap," Collier whispers, almost as if he were witnessing a manifestation of the Flying Spaghetti Monster.

"I wouldn't have expected him to be that bouncy," I say.

"Yeah, you're right. That was actually pretty spectacular," Collier says.

"I hope someone shot video," I say.

"What's going on here?" an angry-sounding voice demands.

And suddenly, I realize a half dozen cops have

surrounded us. They don't go after the kids—I suppose because we're the ones who look out of place at this particular event, meaning we must be the ones who caused the trouble. The cops begin pelting us with all sorts of pointed questions.

"You're in cahoots with Hershey!" Collier raves. He has me worried. If he starts calling the police Nazis, it'll be all over. They'll probably lock us away so deep and for so long that we won't be seen again until archeologists dig us up.

Eventually, I realize the police don't really want to bother with us; they're probably not even sure what, if anything, we might have done that could have been illegal. As level-headed as possible, I promise them we'll pay for the damages, even though it's not our fault, and I'll be responsible for Collier. This belligerent stuff isn't his normal behavior, I tell them (hoping my nose isn't growing as I talk). His goldfish went belly-up this morning, and he's beside himself with grief. Finally, after about a half hour, they run us off the school grounds with explicit, dire warnings not to come back.

***

Collier calls me the next day. Amelia got into the game and was able to give him a detailed report.

"His grandson's on the Sancho Panza team," he tells me. "He plays center. Bill Hershey the Third. Pretty good player, actually. He was in there hustling, knocking guys down and stuff."

"Now are you going to give up the Nazi war criminal stuff? What could be more innocent— what could be more wholesome and All-American—than going to watch your grandson play football?"

"You don't understand these people," Collier says. "Sports are a big part of their plan. Physical fitness. Muscles. They want to achieve domination any way they can."

"Aw, Collier. You know that's ridiculous."

"How can you refuse to face reality like this? Believe me; I understand these people. This is even more conclusive than going to the meeting would have been."

Objections come to mind, but why waste my time? Collier's peculiar brand of logic would allow him to view anything I might say as proof that he's right.

Meanwhile, Collier is still relentlessly pounding away at it. "We need to follow him again," he's saying. "And this time, make sure we get into the game. Amelia did good work, but it'll take a trained eye, like mine, to get the goods on this guy. I'm going to see if I can come up with a miniature camera I can hide inside a shirt button or something. That'll really be handy..."

Special Delivery

I wake to the sounds of bumping and thumping. Lying in bed listening, I think I might be hearing the occasional mild curse as well. Bump, thump, "*Damn.*" Bump, thump, "*Damn.*" And so on.

After a couple minutes, it occurs to me that this is something I should investigate. It might be elves rearranging the living room furniture. It might be demons building an oil derrick in the guest bedroom again.

I roll out of bed, flop onto the floor, and draw myself up on all fours. I shake my head vigorously. I hate getting up.

In the living room, Industrial Waste is clumsily wrestling a large-ish box across the living room floor. All the furniture is out of place, and some knickknacks have fallen from a small shelf unit in one corner. He has somehow managed to knock a couple of pictures off the wall.

"What are you doing?" I ask.

"Help me get this over there, to that spot I cleared out on the floor."

I don't see an area that looks like a cleared-out spot. Regardless, I take a position on the other side of the box and help him shove it to the middle of the room.

"They just delivered it," Industrial says. "It's my new multidimensional pantropic transubstantiating neutrostatic ray gun kit."

"That's quite a fancy name," I say.

"Yeah. It took me an hour and a half to memorize it. I still can't spell it." He whips out his Swiss Army knife and begins slicing away at the packing tape.

"What does it do?"

Industrial makes a couple more slices and raises the flaps to reveal an array of shiny parts nestled into molded Styrofoam packing. Tube-looking parts, electronic-looking parts, motor-looking parts, and so on. "It kills supernatural beings," he says. "Well, I mean, not right now, but when I put it together."

"I see." I'm just being polite, though. I don't see. "Why do you want to do that?"

"For fun." He begins removing parts and laying them out on the floor. Soon, the room looks like Christmas morning for a kid who had asked for a lot of cool-looking, useless junk—but without a Christmas tree. Or wrapping paper. Or Santa Claus passed out drunk in the front yard.

"What kind of supernatural beings?"

Industrial blinks. "Supernatural ones."

"There are lots of kinds of supernatural beings."

"Oh, yeah. Well, ghosts, vampires, werewolves, zombies, mummies, uh..."

"Ghouls?"

"Yeah, ghouls, too."

"Frankenstein monsters?"

"Thor, let me ask you something: Who do you think is the real monster in that story?"

"It's too early in the day to think about stuff like that."

"It's three o'clock in the afternoon." He finds the assembly guide, which is two poorly photocopied sheets stapled together. "I'm going to need a Phillips-head screwdriver and a set of hex keys."

"Why did your order a kit? Why not just get a fully assembled unit?"

"It's against the law to import a fully assembled unit," Industrial says. "Up to a hundred-thousand-dollar fine and/or five years in prison." He looks at the assembly guide. "Okay, first thing is to find the gunstock." He looks over the parts and points. "I think that's it. Grab it for me, will you?"

"That's not a gunstock," I say. "That's a broken-off piece of the television stand I was using five years ago."

But Industrial isn't listening. "Where's the screwdriver?"

***

Later that night, I'm practicing combing my hair when Industrial knocks on my bedroom door. "Hey, Thor," he says, "I'm going out to shoot some vampires. Wanna come along?"

"I don't think so. You go ahead."

"It'll be fun. I've heard that when you hit them, they get this really hilarious look on their faces."

"No. Really, no."

A moment later, a blast of singsongy music comes from next door. Hardison's teenage daughter is having her friends over again, and they're playing this week's Popular, Prefabricated, Synthetic Musical Entertainment Product. I feel as if my ears are turning into plastic.

Those girls might be required by law to listen to that stuff, but as a grown man, I'm not. And I have no intention of doing so. I grab my shoes and run out the back door. In the driveway off the alley, Industrial is loading the gun into his car.

"I've changed my mind," I say. "I want to ride along."

"Sure thing." He lays the gun out along the backseat.

"So that's it, eh?" This is the first time I've seen it fully assembled. It looks like a prop from a low-budget, sixties-era science fiction movie: a bulky thing, sort of like a modified bazooka with lots of dials, buttons, switches, LED displays, meters, and so on.

He gives it an affectionate pat. "Yup. This is it."

"Can you play Tetris on it?"

"I wouldn't be surprised."

"What does it use for ammo?"

"It doesn't need any. It channels the bidirectional protonucleic particles in the operator's aura."

"How long did it take you to memorize that?"

"I haven't yet. I probably got it wrong. I'm sure

it has something to do with your aura, though."

I put on my shoes in the car while Industrial drives. "Is it dangerous to people?" I ask.

"Oh, no, not at all," Industrial says. "The only thing is, if you take a direct hit to the head at close range, there's a forty percent chance that it will create a false memory that you were a member of the 1970 Minnesota Vikings. I don't think that's dangerous, do you?"

"I don't know. I suppose not."

He drives to an industrial area by the riverfront and makes his way through the side streets. He's looking for The Bloody Fang, a bar that caters to vampires. The neighborhood's a good location for it because many of the second-shift factory workers have to walk several blocks in the dark to their cars when they get off. Easy pickins. "I know it's around here somewhere," he says.

I see what looks like a large, bloody fang on top of a low building up ahead. "Is that it?"

"I would say so."

Industrial drives past the place, and we see the sign above the door: THE BLOODY FANG.

A half block down, just on the other side of an underpass, he pulls into the parking lot of a warehouse on the opposite side of the street from the bar. We get out of the car. Industrial looks around to make sure no one's watching. Then he opens the back door and takes out the gun. We walk to the underpass and stand behind a pillar, hidden from the view of anyone at the bar. "I think this looks like a good vantage point," he says. "What do you think?"

"Looks good to me." What do I know? I've never gone vampire hunting.

"Did you bring binoculars?" he asks.

"I was doing well to bring my shoes."

"That's too bad. You really want to be able to see their faces when they get hit." He peeks around the corner of the pillar. "Yeah, this is just right," he says. He raises the gun with crisp, precise motions and peers through the telescopic sight, every bit the SWAT team officer engaged in, maybe, some sort of hostage situation. "Next one that comes out...BAM!"

I stand behind the pillar and look around. It's a good night to be out. The weather is nice, and the sky is clear. The stars spell out BITE ME across the sky. Cool.

And then, after a few moments, Industrial says in a low voice, "Hey, Thor, I see one. Watch this."

I lean around the corner and see a man walk away from the bar toward us. He's dressed in black and wears a long, black cape: the typical vampire look. Industrial says something about "acquiring the target," and then I hear a lame-sounding *click* that sounds sort of like way those old-fashioned toy cap guns sound when you shoot them without caps in them.

The vampire goes down with a fall that almost looks as if his bones suddenly dissolved within him. And then he begins to shrink. I watch as he gets smaller, smaller, smaller...

"He disappeared," I whisper.

"No," Industrial says. "He shriveled up to a little icky thing about the size of a prune. You just can't see it at this distance."

"How do you know? You've never done this before."

"I read about it on the Internet. That's what happens."

"Oh, okay."

"Go look."

I'm curious, but don't want to go look. For some reason, I'm afraid the little icky thing about the size of a prune will be horribly stinky. "You go look."

"I've seen the pictures. *You* go look."

If he doesn't want to go look, there's a reason. "I'll take your word for it," I say.

***

We get home about three o'clock in the morning. Industrial is excited. So am I. He scored a total of three hits, and I got one. We pop open a couple of beers to unwind.

About seven beers later, Industrial says, "Here's what I think."

"What do you think?"

"I think we could use this weapon to kill Satan."

"You might want to reserve judgment on that until a time when you haven't been drinking beer."

"No, I'm serious. The only thing is, Satan isn't one of the presets. So I would have to figure out

how to calibrate the gun for him. But I think it's
doable. I think we could take out the Prince of
Darkness."

I have to admit that it would be the perfect
complement to Stanley Dirndl's petition for a Better America. Still... "Sounds a little ambitious for
a guy who's just been hiding behind a pillar taking
potshots at drunk vampires."

"Think about it. That's all I ask. Think about
it."

***

Industrial spends the next few days hard at work
on his plan. Of critical importance is making sure
the weaponry is just right. The worst possible outcome—a very possible outcome—would be that
the first shot does nothing more than make Satan
mad.

And he, Industrial, is very much aware that
sheer power isn't the only variable. In fact, it isn't
even the most important. He also has to take into
account focus, speed, particle balance and pattern,
wavelength, frequency, and more, much more.

He spends hours and hours and hours poring
over thick books on physics, chemistry, theology,
the occult, and more. He looks up the latitude, lon-
gitude and altitude of the house and graphs the
trends in temperature and humidity in our area.
He reads *Faust* and *The Devil and Daniel Webster*.
He watches dozens of movies like *Damn Yankees*,
Bedazzled, and *Crossroads*.

He decides he needs a second shooter, so he orders another gun.

He talks about building a grassy knoll in the house, but I quash that idea from the outset. He gives me a hurt look, but I hold firm.

One morning I find him passed out in the living room with mathematical formulas written in crayon all over his face. Obviously, this is taking quite a toll on him. When he wakes up, I confront him. "Are you really sure you want to do this?" I ask.

"If we're able to, we owe it to the world."

"*We?*"

The second gun comes, and Industrial recruits Collier Figg as the other gunman—I have to agree that a world without Satan would certainly be a paradise, but I'm not bold enough to actually pull the trigger.

Ah, but Collier—my longtime buddy Collier Figg—takes to it with great gusto and relish. He's ready to dive right in and take some shots at Satan.

The two of them go on several shooting expeditions to familiarize themselves with the guns. As bad as Industrial is with his enthusiasm, Collier is worse, far worse. "You know," he says, "if the first shot stuns him badly enough, I could move in close and gut him with a butcher knife. Imagine that! I could slice Satan's abdomen wide open and pull his entrails out! Feed them to my cat!" This is a side of Collier Figg I haven't seen before, and it's disturbing. (Well, okay. I've seen this side of him before, but it's never been quite this extreme.)

Later, after Collier's gone, I have a word with Industrial. "I'm not so sure I would want him in on this, if it were my project," I say.

"Why not?"

"I think he's going to be a loose cannon. He's talking about gutting Satan with a butcher knife."

"So what?"

"So this: You want your people calm and cool. You want them under control at all times. Industrial, this is going to be very dangerous. You can't have some hothead who's going to be looking for an opening to move in with a butcher knife."

"Oh, pish-posh. He'll be all right."

*   *   *

The plan is to lure Satan into an ambush. The setting will be my kitchen—I want to do it there because I figure there's a good chance this thing could get messy. People could start bleeding. Internal organs could go splat! The easy-to-clean tile floor is the place for all that.

Chickenfeet is going to be the bait. His job is to sit in the kitchen, act hungry, and casually mention that he would be willing to sell his soul to the devil in exchange for a carton of artificially processed cheeselike food product. Satan will appear, contract in one hand and quill pen in the other, ready to prick Chickenfeet's finger for blood to use as ink. And then, while the large, stuffed panda operates the video camera—we have to shoot video, of course—Industrial and Collier will open fire.

(The large, stuffed panda wanted to be the decoy, but as we're not sure whether he has a soul, it seemed advisable to have an actual person do that job. The camera belongs to Chickenfeet, and he was reluctant to let someone else operate it—especially someone with no fingers—but we browbeat him into agreeing by saying stuff like, "Aw, c'mon, be a team player" and "You want to be *one of the guys*, don't you?") And me, I'll be on hand to...well, not to *do* much of anything, but I'll be there simply because it's my house.

Let's say I'm going to supervise.

If all goes well, it'll be over with in less than a minute. And evil? It will be gone.

But then again, if something goes wrong... there's no telling what could happen.

***

We put the plan in motion on a Saturday night. Everyone shows up by six-thirty, and we sit around the living room drinking beer, listening to some of the large, stuffed panda's death metal CDs and working up the courage to get started.

Yeah, beer. That's what we need for this project.

After chugging down his ninth, the large, stuffed panda decides it's time to set up the camera. But he's not much of a drinker. He staggers around, bangs into an end table, and knocks over a floor lamp.

"What are you doing?" I say. "That lamp was a

family heirloom." It wasn't, really.

"I don't think it's damaged," the large, stuffed panda says. He stands there and regards the lamp for a moment and then reaches to pick it up. He slowly topples over on it, throws up, and clumsily rolls around to lie face up, with his head coming to rest in the puddle of vomit.

Well. So much for keeping the icky bio messes off the carpeting. I wonder if the large, stuffed panda is machine washable.

He rouses himself and sits up. "Gee, Thor, I sure am sorry," he says in a raspy voice.

"It's my fault," I say. "I should have known better than to give you beer." It's a good thing he's not going to be one of the shooters.

"Aw, you're so understanding. I'm going to have to send you a fruit basket." He laboriously works his way up to something that resembles a standing position. "I think I'm okay now. I'll go in there and set up." He picks up the camera bag and tripod.

Watching the large, stuffed panda weave around as he leaves the room, Collier Figg kills the rest of his beer and pops another one open. "Yeah, things are getting good," he says.

"You're not going to try to gut Satan with a butcher knife, are you?" I ask.

"Who? Me?"

"I'm not talking to Chickenfeet."

"What makes you think I would try to do something like that? I resent what you're saying, Thor."

"You've already said you wanted to."

"And you took me seriously? I thought you knew me better than that."

Drunk as we both are, I can't be sure whether this is mock outrage or real. I shrug. "Are we ready to go in there?"

Chickenfeet stands up. "I'm ready," he says.

We're unsteady on our feet, but—fortunately—no one is in such bad condition as the large, stuffed panda. We stagger into the kitchen to find him sitting on the floor, intently trying to fit the screw on the tripod into the camera. "I think this is the wrong size," he says.

"It's standard," I say. "It'll fit. Your problem is that you have the camera upside-down." I sit next to him and take the tripod and camera. Looking at the tripod, I quickly find another problem. "You've stripped the threads."

Collier Figg, gun now in hand, turns to me. "How could he do that if he couldn't even get the hole lined up?"

"He's a large, stuffed panda," Industrial Waste says. "You figure it out."

"Hey, c'mon, guys," the large, stuffed panda says, hurt.

"Don't go getting all like that on us," Industrial says. "You know it's true that large, stuffed pandas can't hold their liquor."

"Stereotype much?" Collier Figg says. He doesn't care about defending the large, stuffed panda. He's just instigating.

"Beer's not liquor," Chickenfeet says.

"At least I'm not a short, bitter little man who

makes his living freeloading off of total strangers," the large, stuffed panda says.

"At least I'm not sitting on the floor with my own vomit smeared all over myself," Industrial says.

"Cut it out," I say. "This is going to be dangerous, and we can't be bickering among ourselves." Did I say I was going to supervise? Make that referee. (And let it be said that Industrial isn't normally so mean. But he's what we call, where I come from, "an ornery drunk." Tomorrow, if he remembers any of this, he'll be on the phone to the large, stuffed panda, apologizing and begging forgiveness, professing himself to be a vile, loathsome, contemptible creature unfit to enjoy the society of civilized people. It'll be unseemly. I hope I can be around to overhear his side of the conversation.)

"Yeah, whatever," Industrial says.

Collier Figg says, "Should we adjust our guns?" He raises his and aims at the refrigerator. "Pow, pow." He looks over at Industrial. "Well, come on, man. If I'm going to kill Satan, I need your help."

Industrial shoots him a dirty look. But he just says, "Yeah, let's make the final adjustments." He steps over to the table, where his gun is, and studies the control panel. "First of all, I calculated that we'll need a forty-five degree setting on the asymtropic wave corrector."

"Okay," Collier says.

It looks as if the two are going to be able to work together with no further conflict, so I turn my attention back to the camera. "This thing isn't going to screw on. Chickenfeet, look in the bottom drawer on the far right and see if you can find a roll of duct tape."

Chickenfeet opens the drawer and begins rummaging through it. Finally, he holds up a roll of electrical tape. "This is all I could find," he says.

"Well, that'll have to do."

Forty-five minutes later, our brave shooters have their guns calibrated, and I have the camera taped to the tripod. Chickenfeet sits at the table, leisurely snacking on crackers and knocking back his fourteenth beer. "Do you know what you're going to say?" I ask him.

"Yeah, sure. I'm going to say, 'Daggone it! I would sell my soul for a carton of artificially processed cheeselike food product.'"

With a faint "pop" sound, a man appears next to Chickenfeet. He's tall—the visitor, not Chickenfeet, although Chickenfeet is kinda tall-ish himself—and has a long, pointy nose. His hair is slicked back, and he wears a well-tailored black suit.

He holds a sheet of paper—some sort of antique-looking parchment covered with ornate handwriting—in one hand and a quill pen in the other. "I have a little proposition for you," he says.

"Hey, wait. I wasn't ready," Industrial Waste says. He hurriedly raises his gun and fires. Satan looks around. "C'mon, guys, be cool," he says.

"Oh, crap. I missed."

"Listen," Satan says, "I have a deal—"

"Point-blank range, and you missed," Collier

says. "Some kind of assassin you are."

Angry, Industrial turns and fires at Collier's head. "What the hell?" Collier says. "You're supposed to be shooting at *him*."

"Let me talk," Satan says.

Industrial fires at Satan. This time, Satan gives a little "huff," as if he's been punched not-too-hard in the stomach. "There," Industrial says. "Direct hit." He twists a dial on his gun and fires again.

"Ow! That hurt!" Satan says.

"Take your alpha deflection down about six percent," Industrial says.

Collier runs his finger over a touchscreen and then fires.

"Ow," Satan says. "Stop it!"

"Increase the angle of hyperchromatic convergence by oh-point-oh-oh three degrees," Industrial says.

Industrial and Collier continue shooting and adjusting, adjusting and shooting. Satan dances around as if getting stung repeatedly by a swarm of bees. "C'mon, guys, cut it out! This isn't funny. I'm trying to do something here." And so on. He drops the contract and the pen. The large, stuffed panda, jumping up and down in excitement, knocks the camera over.

Just as I'm beginning to wonder if this is going to do any good, Satan lets out a loud howl and falls to the floor. He doesn't shrivel up into a little icky thing the size of a prune, though. He pukes up a horrid green substance, and a dark, wet stain appears at his crotch. I can smell the distinct odor of pooh.

"We got him now," Industrial says.

Chickenfeet, looking sick, stands up, moaning. "I think I'm going to throw up," he says. I have to admit the stench is indeed sickening beyond belief. I'm having problems myself. Chickenfeet stands up and tries to navigate himself toward the back door, stepping on the video camera along the way.

Collier throws his gun down and picks up a butcher knife from the countertop. He throws his shoulders back and thrusts his chest out. "Yeah, Satan? Yeah? You think you're bad? You want a piece of *this*?"

"Collier, you idiot," I say. I want to step in front of him, but then again, I realize how foolish it would be to get in his way when he's drunk and excited almost to the point of incoherence and itchin' to gut someone with a butcher knife.

"Ugh," Satan says hoarsely.

Chickenfeet, leaning against the refrigerator, throws up.

This isn't going well.

And then, seemingly from nowhere and everywhere, all at once, the sound of a choir singing "AAAAAAAHHHHHH" in a harmony sweeter and more perfect than any you could ever hope to hear on a Queen album fills the room. A baritone voice, full of echo and reverb, booms out: "WHAT'S GOING ON HERE?" It's overdone, in my opinion, but still incredibly effective.

Suddenly, the room is deathly silent. It isn't just the absence of sound. It's as if sound itself has been sucked out of the room. I want to glance around at my friends to see how they're reacting, but I can't move—nothing is preventing me from moving; I'm just scared to appear as anything more than an inanimate object.

A moment later, an angel descends through the ceiling. He has the luminescent white robe, the golden wings, the halo, the whole package. He hovers in the air above the large, stuffed panda. "I'm Gabriel," the angel says.

We still can't say anything. The phone rings. Gabriel looks around at us. No one moves. Finally, the answering machine picks up. "This is Thor. Leave a message. No, not now, you fool! Wait for the beep." *Beep.* "This is Death," a swanky-looking dude dressed in black says, "and I'm—"

Gabriel snatches up the phone. "Listen, you dickless little ball of shit. You're going to stop these calls *this very instant*. You're nothing special. It takes no talent or imagination to do what you do. The only reason we hired you to be Death was because you said you had your own weapons, and it turned out that all you had was a piece of wood with a nail in it. Now stop bothering people and *do your fucking job!*"

Gabriel slams the phone down. He pauses for a beat—timing is everything—and heaves a sigh. "As I was saying, I'm Gabriel. *And I asked*: What's going on here?"

Industrial finds his tongue. "We...we were trying to kill Satan."

"And whose idea was this?"

Everyone points at Industrial. Industrial points at Collier Figg.

"Why?"

"Well," Industrial says, "we, uh...we figured it would rid the world of evil." The room, once again, is quiet for several agonizing moments. "That would be a good thing, wouldn't it?"

Gabriel heaves a weary sigh. He floats over to Satan and helps him sit up, and then he grabs a dish towel. He kneels next to Satan and wipes off his face. "Look at me," Gabriel says. He takes Satan's chin in his hand and tilts his head up. He gives Satan a couple of slaps on the cheek and peers into his eyes. He makes the old "V for Victory" sign. "How many fingers am I holding up?"

Satan's mouth opens, but the only sounds he can make are coughing and gacking noises. Thick, ochre-colored drool oozes from the corner of his mouth. He holds up two shaky fingers.

"Good. Can you feel this?" Gabriel asks. He pinches Satan's arm. Satan jerks away.

Gabriel turns to face the rest of us. "Who lives here?"

"I do," I say.

"Do you have vitamin C tablets?"

"I don't have vitamin *anything*. Dude, a couple of straight, single guys live here. We stuff ourselves full of pizza, donuts, beer, and not much else."

"I had a can of pickled chrysanthemum kidneys in fortissimo sauce yesterday," Industrial says.

"Did you put garlic on them?" the large, stuffed panda asks. "Put garlic on them, and they're to *die* for."

"Shut up," Gabriel says. And then, to me, "Do you have orange juice?"

"Actually, we might." I start toward the refrigerator, but then I see the orange puddle on the floor. The video camera is in the middle of it, covered in a nice-looking glaze. The carton lies on its side at the edge of the puddle, just behind the outstretched arm of the large, stuffed panda, juice still dripping from its spout. The camera lens, cracked, glimmers at me.

Gabriel shakes his head sadly. "You people are disgusting." He turns back to Satan. "Listen. You're going to be all right. In just a minute, I'm going to send you back to hell. Understand?"

Satan nods.

"Get some vitamin C into your system," Gabriel says. "As much as you can. Stay in bed for a couple days and keep warm. Will Hortense be home?"

Collier Figg snickers. "Hortense?"

Gabriel looks up and points at him. Collier staggers back a step, as if Gabriel actually poked him in the chest. "You, shut up," Gabriel says, and then he turns back to Satan. "Will she be home?"

Satan nods weakly.

"Good. She'll take care of you. Why did you walk into an ambush like that?"

Satan coughs and sputters. "I...ack...didn't think those guns...cough, cough...would work ...blecccchhh...I thought I...ack...could..."

"All right, don't strain yourself. We'll talk about it later."

"Gack."

"Remember what I told you, right? Lots of vitamin C, and stay in bed for a couple days."

Satan nods.

"Good. Now, back to hell with you!" Gabriel waves his hand, and Satan disappears.

Gabriel stands up. "As for the rest of you: Don't ever, ever, *ever* try a stunt like this again."

"But—" Industrial says.

"There's no 'but' about it. Leave him alone."

"But evil..." Industrial says. "Temptation."

"There's no evil," Gabriel says. "There's no *need* for evil. There's only human greed and stupidity."

We stand around gaping at Gabriel, uncomprehending.

"Look," he says, "no one, Satan included, has any interest in luring people into sin just for the sake of sending them to hell. That would be a dick move, don't you think?"

"Well, then...like, what does Satan do?"

"He's an administrator. A prison warden. And a damn good one, I might add. We don't need people attacking him."

"But what about the contract?" Chickenfeet asks.

"What contract?"

Chickenfeet points to the parchment on the floor. "To buy my soul."

Gabriel gives him a withering look. "Look, I don't know what that thing says, but he doesn't have to buy souls. He doesn't *want* to. The fewer people who get damned, the easier his job is.

If everyone went to Heaven, he could sit around drinking beer and watching Bruce Willis movies all the time."

I have to admit that that sounds pretty good.

Chickenfeet picks up the contract and wipes a few chunks of vomit off of it with his sleeve. He moves his lips as he reads. After a moment, he clears his throat. "Well," he says, "there's no mention of a soul here. It would seem he was going to offer me a carton of artificially processed cheese-like food product in exchange for videotaping his wedding."

"Huh?" Industrial says.

"Yeah. Next Saturday."

"There," Gabriel says. "See? And, might I add, his fiancé—*Hortense*—is a very lovely young lady. None of you sorry losers could hope to bag a babe that hot."

"Hey, you don't know..." Collier says, angry.

"Now, if you'll excuse me, I have to get back to the office. I'm taking delivery of a new desk today." He looks upward, raises his arms, and then stops and looks around the room. "You people need to grow up."

With that, the heavenly chorus sings another impossibly harmonious chord, and Gabriel ascends through the ceiling.

"You know what?" Collier says as the chord fades away to nothingness. "This reminds me of the time when I was with the Vikings, and it was halftime during the Lions game..."

Solitaire America, Part 3

I open my eyes, eager to face the day. It's June 12, the day Stanley Dirndl's Better America is set to begin. It'll be a day of hope, a day of wonderment. It'll be the best day of all time in every American's life, including mine.

Sitting up in bed, I notice that nothing seems to be different. My room is still just my room. Nonetheless, that doesn't mean America isn't better. No, it doesn't mean that at all. The real test will be...what?

The real test will be the news. I go to industrial's door and give it a good, spirited knock. "Come on out and watch TV," I say.

"Huh?"

I open the door and step inside. "The news," I say. "We have to watch the news."

"Why?"

"Today is the first day of a better America," I say. "We need to check it out."

"Yes. Yes, you're right." Industrial rolls out of bed. "We need popcorn for this," he says.

***

Ten minutes later, we have a huge bowl of popcorn on the sofa between us, and I have the remote in hand. "Ready?" I ask.

"Sure thing, Thor."

I point the remote at the TV. "Prepare yourself, my friend, for the majesty of a better America." With that, I mash the on button down. I try to make a grand ritual of it, but pressing a button isn't much of a ritual under any circumstances.

The television comes to life. I hit the channel button a few times and find the Legitimate Information and Editorial Station. We stuff handfuls of popcorn gluttonlike into our mouths and watch.

One by one, the stories unfold...

A writer was found shot to death in washed-up movie star's swimming pool.

A pinball camp was trashed by riots.

A guy's rug was stolen.

"This stuff shouldn't be happening," Industrial says.

"No, it shouldn't."

A scientist's DNA got mixed up with a housefly's.

"Aw, that's some grotesque shit," Industrial says. "I'm talking about re*pug*nant."

Birds attacked a small town.

"What's going on here?" I say.

We watch, puzzled, as story after story of tragedy and evil unfold before us. This can't be happening, but there it is nonetheless. And then, it occurs to me: the answer lives just around the corner. "C'mon."

I fly out the door, with Industrial following. "Where are we going?" he asks.

"To find out what went wrong." I run down the street, fully expecting to find Stanley Dirndl trembling with rage, angry to the point of incoherence that he had been sold out, double-crossed, betrayed. My guess is that someone very powerful, somewhere, somehow, for some reason, had an interest in keeping America from getting better. It's probably about money. Ultimately, it's always about money.

***

Industrial and I make our way down Festerville Road to the old Used Tennis Ball Exchange storefront, and I knock on the door.

Stanley answers in a bathrobe. He's not at all enraged. In fact, he moves about lackadaisically, and his face has the bleary look of someone who just woke up. "Stanley," I say, "what went wrong? Why is America not better?"

"Huh?"

Could it be he's not aware that there's no change? Surely not! Surely he would have been up at the crack of dawn to enjoy the wonderfulness of the Better America that he, had things gone right, would have brought about. "The better America!" I shout at him. "It was supposed to start today, but it didn't."

"Oh, that." He digs in his ear and grimaces. "Well, I can tell you about that. Come in."

Industrial and I step inside, and everyone sits down on office chairs that look as if they were salvaged from a junkyard. "So what's the story?" Industrial asks.

Stanley heaves a deep sigh. "See, it's like this: I got the letter telling me that my request was approved. They were going to make America better."

"Right, right," I say.

"And I got all excited and started telling everyone I could about it."

"I know. We saw you on TV."

"Yes. TV interviews," Dirndl says. "Magazine articles. Better America merchandising. Do you have any conception of how many offers I got for official Better America merchandise?"

I had never thought about it, but it seemed only natural. Better America calendars, Better America T-shirts, Better America frozen vegetables, and so on. "I suppose you were inundated," I say.

"I was. The offer for Official Stanley Dirndl Better America ocarinas was lucrative beyond belief," he said.

"I would buy one," Industrial said.

"That's exactly what I'm talking about. A Better America reality show. This idea of a better America—everyone thought it was great."

"It would have been," I say.

"I'm not so sure."

"Why not?"

"It was too easy," Dirndl says. "I started

thinking about it: fill out some paperwork, and all of a sudden they're going to make America better. What am I supposed to think about that?"

"I'm afraid I don't see a problem," Industrial says.

"Like I said, it was too easy. If that's all it takes, why hasn't anyone done it before?"

I shrug. Industrial shrugs. Who cares? It's being done now. Or, that is to say, it *was* being done until recently. Isn't that good enough? Wasn't it? Wouldn't it have been?

Stanley goes on. "There had to be a catch. There had to be some sinister—some very, very sinister angle to this that I wasn't seeing."

"I don't see why you would think that," I say.

"Yeah. Better is better," Industrial says. "What's not to like about that?"

"Better is better, yes. But for who?" Stanley asks.

"Whom," I correct.

"It's like promising to give someone a computer and giving them an old typewriter instead," Stanley says.

"What?"

"Okay, maybe it's not. But it sort of felt like it. So I went back and told them I didn't want the better America after all."

"You did that?" I ask.

"More or less. But it's not really that simple. More paperwork, and so on. It took me three weeks to fill out all the paperwork. All sorts of forms and applications. And the filing fees. It's insane, quite insane. But I had to do it." Dirndl pauses and looks me square in the eye. "You understand, don't you?"

"I...I don't know. I think I do." I don't believe he would have gone to all that trouble if he wasn't sure about what he was doing. Even if he was wrong about everything, he must have felt sure of himself.

"I assure you," Dirndl says, "if there had been any other way...any other way at all..."

I stand up, not sure whether to shake his hand or choke him to death. Considering that America hasn't been made better, choking certainly remains an option. Ah, but what would be the point? "You did what you had to do," I tell him. "That's all we can expect of anyone."

"I'm glad you understand." Dirndl stands up and walks to the door with us. "But you know, just because I couldn't follow through with it doesn't mean it can't happen. Maybe someone else will take the bull by the horns and circulate another petition."

"That sounds like a good project for Industrial," I say. "He could hire some people to help out and equip them with laptop computers."

Industrial punches me on the arm.

"Don't," I say. I open the door and hear music off at a distance.

As Industrial and I step outside, a late model, forest green Universal Motors Ferret LSD four-door coupe pulls up to the curb. The windows are down, and the music, which I now recognize as KC and the Sunshine Band's "I'm Your Boogie Man," is blasting out, preposterously loud. Even across thirty feet of wide-open, empty parking lot, it's oppressive.

And something nags at me: I could swear I've seen this car before, but I can't remember where.

Behind me, Dirndl says, "Is the sun stuck again?" He has to shout.

"I don't know," I say. Apart from the onslaught of noise, I find the car worrisome. I start to search my memory. But then the driver looks toward us, and I see that he's none other than Full Metal Thermostat! He reaches across the passenger seat and aims the young lover's gun in our direction. Instinctively, I turn to go back inside just in time to see Stanley Dirndl's head disappear in a spectacular explosion of pink mist.

Tires squeal, and Metal is gone.

Industrial and I stand around for several minutes in front of the open door, wide-eyed and speechless, trying to figure out if what we saw was really what happened. I look inside and see bone, blood, and brains all over the room. Stanley's headless body is sprawled on the floor in an awkward position. It's messy. Very, very messy.

"Wow," Industrial finally says. "Nice shot." His voice is nothing more than a pitiful croak, as if he has just eaten a large serving of sixty-grit sandpaper (and maybe he has, for all I know).

"Industrial, I'm inclined to think it's best if we were never here."

The idea seems to surprise him as much as the shooting did. "Yeah," he says.

We walk a couple of blocks in silence, hoping we don't look suspicious, and round the corner. Industrial heads over to a bus stop and sits on the bench. "You know," he says, "it's going to take us ages to figure out what's been going on and how it all fits together."

"I'm not even going to try."

***

Back home, I see that we left the TV on. Industrial and I watch a news segment about a computer that staged a mutiny on an interplanetary spaceship.

If you liked *Soft White Underbelly*, try these other books by Ray Holland:

The Hermit: A dedicated career hermit becomes mixed up with a promiscuous young lady from a nearby village in this kinda-sorta parable-fairy-tale-type story. Who, if anyone, lives happily ever after?

Goliath: It's a tale of good and evil, of trust and suspicion, of the power of love and loyalty. Little Goliath and his friends face adversity from within themselves, from one another, and from the forces of evil as they work to foil the Neuralgia Sisters' nefarious plot to achieve world domination.

Open Stage: A mysterious, alluring woman, a hyperactive, funny little man, and a very strange business deal leads Gilbert Ragwater to learn a few things about himself. It's a coming-of-age story for those of us with arrested development.

The Hookie-Pookie Man: His mother was from Earth, and his father was from another planet. He doesn't fit in anywhere, but he knows a woman of similar origin is out there somewhere—and he's determined to find her.